I0668863

AIRSHIP 27 PRODUCTIONS

C.O. Jones: Hometown—U.S.A. © 2021 Fred Adams Jr.

Published by Airship 27 Productions
www.airship27.com
www.airship27hangar.com

Interior and cover illustrations © 2021 Rob Davis

Editor: Ron Fortier
Associate Editor: Gordon Dymowski
Marketing and Promotions Manager: Michael Vance
Production designer: Rob Davis.

All rights reserved under International and Pan-American Copyright Conventions. No part of this book may be reproduced in any manner without permission in writing from the copyright holder, except by a reviewer, who may quote brief passages in a review.

ISBN: 978-1-953589-07-1

Printed in the United States of America

10 9 8 7 6 5 4 3 2 1

C.O. JONES
HOMETOWN—U.S.A.

BY FRED ADAMS JR.

I

KANSAS 18 October 1949

Driving across Kansas was something C.O. Jones had done once before and he hoped that once this trip was over, he wouldn't have to do it again. Dusty roads disappeared into the horizon like a runway fifty miles at a stretch with nothing to see on either side but those amber waves of grain hometown patriots sing about at Rotary Club meetings.

Danny Hayes, the reason Jones was making the dreary drive through that place at that time sat slumped in the passenger seat, blissfully asleep. Hayes had shown up in Los Angeles four days before to bring Jones back to Brownsville, Pennsylvania at the request of his former employer, mobster Skitch Mottola.

"Skitch needs you," was all Danny had to say. Jones owed Skitch, and it was a good time to go back to Brownsville. He'd made a decent living as a private eye and bounty hunter for a few years out West, but he had run afoul of the LAPD and the Feds one time too many, and the City of Angels had gotten too hot for him to stick around. They could have taken the train, but Jones wouldn't give up his car, a '41 Ford coupe set up to outrun anything on four wheels and with more tricks built into it than Houdini's stage show. Like a cowboy's faithful horse, the Ford went with Jones.

The car was running well but it looked like it had been through a war, which on a small scale, it had. Jones and Danny kept the windows rolled down so the jagged holes in the glass didn't show, but there wasn't enough time to do anything about the .30 caliber holes punched in the door and one fender.

The drive was hot, dusty, and tedious. He had seen only two cars and a farm truck pulling a wagon overflowing with hay going the other way in the last two hours. When they'd passed the wagon, Danny licked his thumb and wiped it in his palm.

"What was that for?" Jones asked.

"Old Irish superstition. When you pass a load of hay on the road, you lick your thumb, wipe it in your palm, and make a wish. You oughta try it."

"What'd you wish for?"

"That I was back in Pennsylvania."

"That'll come true soon enough."

The state of Kansas was four hundred miles long, and Jones was determined to get through it as fast as he could before the monotony of the landscape put him to sleep and he drove off the highway and the Ford was swallowed by the endless fields of wheat. When he looked in his rear view mirror and saw the flashing light of a police car, he almost welcomed the diversion. He elbowed Danny. "Wake up. We have company."

Jones pulled to the side of the road. He could have outrun the cops, but they probably had a radio in the car, and they could signal ahead. He'd rather deal with whoever was in the cop car than have half the Kansas Highway Patrol waiting for them at a roadblock. Jones opened his door and stepped out, blinking in the bright sun. He pulled down the brim of his hat to shade his eyes. He could hear the siren now as the car got closer.

The police car, a black and white '37 Pontiac, pulled up behind Jones's Ford. An old car, thought Jones. Detroit was still playing catch-up with the postwar demand for new ones. Two uniformed patrolmen climbed out. They wore khaki shirts with sewn creases and epaulettes, dark trousers with a stripe down each leg, and campaign hats. Neither one had a ticket pad in his hand.

The driver, an older veteran of the force, wore that tired look that all cops get after twenty years of the life. The other, a short fellow walked with the bounce of a bantam rooster. His boots were spit shined, and so was the black Sam Browne belt over his khaki tunic. Jones guessed he was about twenty-two and spent the war stateside; he still had something to prove.

"Afternoon, officers," Jones said, hands hanging loosely at his sides. No threat.

"Do you know how fast you were going?" the short one said, the tone of his voice teetering between authority and arrogance.

Jones shrugged. "I'm not sure. The speedometer doesn't read past a hundred."

"A smart one, huh?" The little cop sneered. "You think this is funny, fella?" The palm of his hand dropped to the pommel of his Billy club.

"Where'd you serve?" Danny said.

The short cop glared at Danny. "None of your business."

"Just wondering," Danny said, tucking a cigarette into the corner of his mouth. "I fought at Anzio."

"Well this ain't Anzio, pal." He took his Billy from his belt and strutted around Jones, eyeing him up and tapping the club in his palm. "How about this?" The cop rapped at the bullet holes in the front fender. "Where'd those come from?" He stepped in front of Jones. "Maybe you two are running from something, huh?" He shot over his shoulder, "What do you think, Ray?"

The older cop said, "I guess we'll find out, Jerry. Let's see your driver's license, buddy."

"Sure thing." Jones nodded. He reached for the wallet in his hip pocket and felt a twinge at the base of his brain. The vision he called the Sight showed Jerry swinging his nightstick. Jones ducked and the Billy whistled over his head. He stepped in and slipped his arm up to the elbow under the rookie's shoulder and twisted his torso, throwing Jerry over his hip and slamming him onto the pavement. Jones kicked the nightstick away and it rolled in a crescent path off the road.

Ray's hand was dropping to his pistol when Jones snapped his left arm straight and a stubby .32 revolver slid from his sleeve into his palm, aimed at Ray's forehead. Ray froze. Jones rose to a crouch. "If I was going for a weapon, I wouldn't be reaching in my back pocket. All this punk wanted was an excuse to hit somebody."

"I—I" Jerry stammered. His eyes were wide with fear.

"Shut your mouth while you still can." He nodded to Danny. "Disarm the officers."

Jones's professional tone chilled Ray. For the first time, fear showed in the older patrolman's face. "Listen, son, we can work this out. We aren't past the point where — "

"You too. Shut it." Jones stood and put the arch of his boot over Jerry's throat. Danny had his automatic out now. He stepped behind Ray and slid his service revolver from its holster. He crouched over the young cop and took his pistol too.

"Look in the car, see what you find." Jones hadn't moved since the revolver appeared.

Danny climbed into the patrol car. The radio under the dash spewed static and squawking voices. A .12 gauge riot gun was clipped to the dashboard, aimed at the car's roof. Danny jacked out the shells and dropped them in his pocket.

He pulled the radio mic from its cradle and yanked the cable from the unit. He got out and called to Jones. "Tires?"

Jones shook his head. "No, we have to leave these two a ledge to stand on. Drain the radiator."

Danny crawled under the car and opened the drain cock. In a minute, the radiator was dry.

"How far to the state line?" Jones asked Ray.

The older cop's eyes avoided Jones's stare. "Twenty miles."

Jones emptied their pistols and threw the bullets to one side of the road and the guns into the monolithic wall of wheat on the other. He reached into his pocket and pulled out a roll of bills. He peeled two fifties off the outside with his thumb. He tucked the money into the breast pocket of Ray's blue uniform. "Have a nice day."

As Danny and Jones climbed back into the Ford, Ray blurted, "Who the hell are you guys?"

Jones looked back and gave him a cold smile. "Veterans."

As they drove away, Jones looked in the rear view mirror and saw Ray helping the young cop to his feet. The little guy was flapping his arms and pointing after them.

"Why'd you give them the money?"

"Think of it as a lesson in public relations, Danny. As it stands, they can save face with their chief and the Department. They can write this off as a day when everything went wrong; the radiator sprung a leak, the radio was on the fritz, and they were stuck.

"Neither of them, especially the rookie wants to admit he got his ass kicked and his weapon taken away. They'll find their guns and somebody will come along to get them water for the radiator. By then, we'll be out of the state and out of their jurisdiction. I don't think either of them will want to turn over a hundred bucks to their chief, especially when the whole point of them stopping us was to shake us down. They'll keep the money and shut up. The little hothead won't like it, but the old cop will make him see the light. Bottom line, nobody comes after us."

"Do me a favor."

"What's that?"

"When we get to Missouri, slow down to eighty."

II

A day later, the landscape changed from the rolling plains to a panorama of mountains that looked as if somebody had kicked up a dark green carpet and left it rumpled at the end of a hallway. The day after, through

Kentucky and into West Virginia, the arid weather was replaced by a driving rain that hammered the roof of the car, strained its windshield wipers, and blew through the jagged holes in the windows.

They stopped for gas at a rickety shack perched on the edge of an overlook. The wind threatened to push the ramshackle pile of lumber over the cliff and into the valley below. Beside two warped picnic tables, a sign proudly proclaimed: Lookout Point – The Best View in West Virginia. Jones pulled up beside two rusted pumps with hand cranks that looked like robots from the cover of some science fiction pulp.

Danny peered out the window. "If that's the best view in West Virginia, I'd hate to see the rest of the state."

Jones laughed. "I suppose it looks a lot better when the sun's out."

Jones tooted the horn and an old man darted out of the shack bobbing and weaving as if he could run between the drops that fell like buckshot. The hood of his yellow rain slicker blew off his head every time he tried to pull it back up. Jones rolled down his window. "Fill it."

"Regular or Ethyl?" The dirty pink of his tongue showed between his missing teeth.

"Give me the best you got."

The old man cackled and said, "Yes, sir."

"I'm out of cigarettes," Danny said, then called to the old man. "You got cigarettes inside?"

"Sure do. Cigarettes, beer, soda pop, whatever you need."

Danny put his hat on. "I'll get us some smokes. You want anything else?"

"Naah, I'm just going to the can."

The codger was cranking the handle and pumping gas for all he was worth to get it over with and get back inside out of the rain. Jones climbed out of the car and started for the pair of outhouses, one for men, one for women, apart from the shack. Planted in front of them was a sign crudely painted in red letters: Whites Only."

Jones balled his fists as he thought about Isaac Jacobs, the blind vet who worked for him in L.A. and about the love of his life, Deanna Drake, the Jamaican chanteuse he'd lost years before to a German bomb on a Soho street . He grabbed the sign with both hands and looked over his shoulder at the old man. He wanted the bigot to turn and look at him, to see what he was doing, but the old cracker was too busy making money, and the rain was falling too hard. Jones yanked the sign out of the ground and sent it pinwheeling over the edge and into the trees below.

He climbed back into the car, and in a minute the old man was at his window. "She was purt' near empty. That'll be four dollars and twenty-one cents." He held out a hand that arthritis was turning into a claw.

Jones handed him a five. "Keep the change."

"Thanks, Mister. From California, huh?"

Jones rolled up the window, shutting off the conversation. It was time to change the license plate. Danny piled in and Jones pulled out, leaving the old man standing in the rain clutching the soggy five dollar bill, his slicker flapping around his legs.

"Twenty six cents a gallon," Danny read from the sandwich board sign at the edge of the lot. "Never gets any cheaper does it?"

"No, but at least it isn't rationed anymore."

Danny chuckled. "Never seemed to be a problem for Skitch. He never seemed to run out of stamps for himself or the boys."

Jones thought of the line of big fancy Cadillacs and Packards he'd seen every day in front of Skitch's poolroom in Snowden Square. No, none of those cars would ever have run dry. Not while there were pickups and pay-offs to be made. Not while there was money to be made.

What must the average working stiff have thought as the mobsters rolled past them while they walked ten miles to the mine or the mill. He shrugged off the thought and focused on the rain-black ribbon of road that stretched ahead of them. Tomorrow the ride would be over.

Jones slept while Danny drove through the winding roads of West Virginia, and as they often did, the dreams came. His name was Randall Simmons during the war, a raw recruit sweating in the sun at Fort Claiborne, one of a couple of thousand men standing in formation on the parade ground in the Louisiana heat and humidity.

From 1939 through 1946 a half million soldiers were trained at Claiborne, and the new enlistee was being stamped by the same die as all of them. With his hair sheared to the scalp and his body clad in the identical green fatigues of his fellows, if someone held a giant mirror in front of the group, he couldn't have found himself in the ranks unless he raised his hand over his head and waved.

But that was the point. Strip men of their individuality so that in combat they would think of their units and not of themselves. America is an institution whose basic unit is the individual. The United States Army is an institution whose basic unit is the squad. All are equally valuable, all are equally expendable; none is special. Then without warning, Private Randall Simmons became very special.

"Atten-hut!" The Sergeant-Major shouted, and the ranks snapped to. A full colonel stepped out of a Jeep and with him, a withered crone in a black dress and shawl, little more than rags. The pair walked down one line after another, looking forward as they went, the Colonel stiff-spined, the woman curved like a claw, never making eye contact with the soldiers.

She stopped and tugged at the Colonel's elbow, turned, and pointed a gnarled finger at Simmons. Her cataract-blue eye met his, and a chill wrapped around his heart. "That one. Him." The woman, he later learned, was Madame Lavois, a Cajun witch from the bayou, and she had tagged him as "special" for Colonel Reynald Hennessey.

Since he was a boy, Randall Simmons had experienced what he came to know as the "Sight," an ability to see things a second or two before they happened, and it qualified him for a special unit in the OSS. "Do you believe in magic, the supernatural, son?" Hennessey had asked him at the outset.

"Ghosts and witches and such? No, sir, I can't say that I do."

"Adolph Hitler does, and he's got the S.S. scouring Europe for artifacts, books of spells, rituals, locations of magical force, and he plans to use them to win this war. It is our job to hinder that acquisition and application to the highest degree possible."

To that end, Randall Simmons, suddenly a lieutenant was tested, and then he was trained. His education was comprehensive on three fronts. He was taught more ways to kill than perhaps there were enemies and taught to operate every weapon and piece of equipment on both sides of the Atlantic to equip him for conventional warfare. Then he was given special instruction at the Mysterious Camp X in Canada to ready him for espionage. Last, he was educated in the rudiments of magic and prepared for a completely different kind of war.

"This is no battle of Good against Evil," Hennessey told him. "Magic is like chemistry or physics. Certain activity yields specific results within the known universe. It becomes an issue of fighting smart instead of fighting hard. What we take from them, diminishes their effectiveness and enhances ours, making victory more likely. It's what you might call a 'zero-sum game.'"

"And if we lose, sir?" Simmons said.

"We dare not lose."

IV

Brownsville was an oddity, one of the most prosperous towns in early America, seated at an intersection of U.S. Route 40, the National Road, and the Monongahela River, two of the most used routes for the transport of goods and people in the original thirteen states. It was once believed that Pittsburgh would never amount to much because it was too close on the river to Brownsville. But the wheel turns in a century and a half, and had it not been for the coal and coke industry, Brownsville's sun would have set decades before.

The wartime demand for both to make steel in Pittsburgh's mills pulled the adjoining counties back from the Depression in the short run, but the town was slowly withering on the vine as the economy shifted its focus. One thing that remained unchanged, however, was organized crime. The local operations still ran like medieval fiefdoms in the Western Counties, and Brownsville was no exception.

Jones woke as the Ford rolled down the long hill into Brownsville. He had been gone only two years, but as they drove through Market Street, he could see the telltale signs of decay creeping around the edges of the once booming town; a shop closed here, an unpainted storefront gone shabby there, and men loitering on the street, out of work with nothing to do.

Danny parked the car across from a four-story building with the word Pool on the broad front windows. "Welcome back, Jonesey."

Jones climbed out of the car, stiff from the ride. Danny threw him the keys, and the pair crossed the street to the pool hall's entrance. One thing hadn't changed: the Packards and Cadillacs still lined the street in a show of affluence and power. At the end of the row sat a cherry red '49 Ford convertible. The chromed bomb in the grille, a cross between a cone and a sphere, poked out like an artillery shell from the mouth of a gun, a warning to get out of the way.

"That Dodie's new car?" Jones pointed to the convertible.

"Yep," Danny said. "Got tired of the Mercury. I hear this one's pretty fast. Got a flathead V-8. He took a page from your book and had Coakee soup up the engine for him."

"He could have picked a more subtle color."

Danny shrugged. "You know Dodie."

They stepped through the door from the cold autumn air into the pool room, and Jones was so quickly immersed in the atmosphere that it felt as if he had never left. A blue haze of cigarette smoke hung between the green table tops and the chain lamps over each. All of the tables were busy but the one in the corner farthest from the door. Skitch's private table stood with a canvas shroud over it and the lamp dark.

"Hey, Danny; hey, Jones." Bucky called out over the crack of the balls and cries of exultation from some shooters and profanity from others. Bucky was named, probably from childhood for his teeth. He wasn't too bright, but he was as loyal to Skitch as the family dog. His long arms poked past the wrists from the sleeves of a shirt he probably hadn't changed twice since VJ Day.

"Hey, Bucky," Danny said, "ring upstairs and tell Skitch we're here, okay?"

He nodded, a forelock of his greasy hair swinging side to side. "Sure thing, Danny."

Jones's eye drifted to the thrones, the tall high-backed chairs that lined the wall opposite the windows. Jack Mozzo, Skitch's partner raised a hand in greeting. The locals called Mozzo "Jackie the Leg," because of his prosthesis, a hollow leg from the knee down where he carried the operation's money. "Safer than a safe," he once told Jones, "'cause a safe don't shoot back." Beside him, Salvatore Figgio, his driver and bodyguard sat watching the room, his eyes sweeping it like a prison yard spotlight.

Bucky shambled over. When he walked, his chin made a scooping motion, as if he were digging, to the left when he raised his left foot, and then to the right. The effect was comical, but nobody in the pool room made fun of him. He might be a dog, but he was Skitch's dog.

"Go on up, guys," Bucky said. "Elevator's waiting."

Jones and Danny climbed the stairs, and the odor of cigarettes and talc was replaced with the smell of sweat and leather. The second floor was a boxing gym where local fighters trained on their way up and trained others on their way down. A gang of men, some in gym clothes and some in suits and suspenders, were gathered around the ring watching two boxers spar, one a rangy blonde kid, and the other, a more compact black man with hair the color and texture of rusted steel wool.

"New blood," Danny said over the shouts of the rubberneckers as they stopped to watch. "The white boy's Billy French from Uniontown. The black fella's Red Jefferson. He's from Cardale. Fats Mungo brought the two of them here on the same day. Says he's gonna make middleweight champs out of both of them. I don't see how that's gonna happen, though, since they're both in the same weight class. There can only be one winner."

"At a time," Jones said.

In the ring the young men were slugging it out, and despite the heavy sparring gloves, both were landing hard body blows and rattling each other's brains under the headgear. French used his reach to try to keep Red at bay, but Red would dance in and punish French's ribs before the white boxer would tag Red with a hook that knocked him back a step.

On the sideline, Fats Mungo bellowed in his hoarse phlegmy voice. His thick jowls waggled as shouted at both fighters at once. "Yeah, get inside that left. Use your right. Oh for Chrissakes, keep your guard up; you want him to kill you?"

"He doesn't use names. How does either one know who he's coaching when?"

"Damned if I know," Danny said.

The bell rang and the fighters broke then clapped their arms around each other in a quick embrace and climbed out of the ring, tossing friendly barbs at each other.

"That's a good sign," Jones said. "They leave it in the ring."

"Yeah," Danny said. "I hope they keep it that way. C'mon. Skitch is waiting."

The stairs to the upper two floors were walled off and the only way to reach them was an elevator in the back corner of the gym. Buckshot, Skitch's bouncer and bodyguard stood waiting beside the open cage. Buckshot was six-and-a-half feet of hard muscle, a prize fighter's build capped with a face cratered by smallpox scars, the origin of his nickname. The bouncer nodded and stepped back to let them into the elevator.

The car rose, and as they passed the third floor, through the open cage, Jones and Danny saw six men at a round table playing cards. A mound of money was heaped in the middle of the table, and a pair of men circled it like sharks, watching for cheats. A young man in a hundred-dollar suit and wearing a pomaded hairdo and wire rimmed glasses dealt the cards.

"How did Skitch get Joey Ice away from Little Johnny?" Jones said.

"Money talks." Danny chuckled. "People got scared off after Armenian Sam showed up in the river for trying to work Johnny's game. No players, no money. Joey's a whore. Next person who offers him five dollars more, he'll tell Skitch goodbye."

The cage stopped at the fourth floor. Most of it was a big room taken up with long tables piled with "policy" slips from the day's numbers game. Jones followed Danny through the tables where half a dozen men were busily sorting the slips into a thousand neat piles. A tote board with the race results from Pimlico took up one wall, and in a corner, Richie Traficante sat at his desk talking on two or three of seven telephones at once while he watched the big board.

Opposite the elevator, Skitch's office door stood ajar, and Dodie, Skitch's brother and partner, stood in the doorway. Dodie was a larger version of Skitch, sharing his facial features and blue-black beard shadow as siblings do, but while his older brother favored three-piece suits and silk Foulard neckties, Dodie wore pointy shoes, pegged pants, and brightly colored shirts like the hep cats from L.A. His dark hair swirled in a duck's ass and pushed downward into a pair of sideburns that stopped at his earlobes.

Dodie turned his head and said something over his shoulder as Jones and Danny approached. When they got to the door, he stepped back and waved them inside.

As soon as the door shut, the hubbub from the floor stopped. Soundproofed, Jones thought, a good idea considering the conversations that go on in here. Unlike the rest of the building, Skitch's office was carpeted in a thick-piled maroon. Floor length drapes covered the windows, and on the wall he saw a painting of a city that Jones recognized as Florence.

"You changed the painting," Jones said. "Last time I was here, it was Venice."

Skitch sat in vest and shirt sleeves behind a dark mahogany desk so shiny you almost expected its surface would ripple if you touched it. "A change of scenery once in a while does a fellow good."

Skitch was a short man, but well proportioned, athletic like a gymnast. Unlike Dodie, he was beginning to go bald, his hairline an inch further back since Jones had last seen him. The burden of the crown, Jones thought, as Skitch stood and offered his hand across the desktop for Jones to shake. His grip was as hard as ever. "Good that you're here, Jones." He motioned to the chairs, and Jones and Danny sat. Dodie closed the door and slouched against it, arms crossed.

"How's Frankie?" Jones said. Two years before, Jones had rescued Skitch's five-year-old son from kidnappers who wanted to exploit the boy's fledgling precognition.

Skitch smiled broadly. "The kid's in the second grade and he reads better than I do already."

"The Missus?"

"Good, good." Skitch would have returned the courtesy, but he knew Jones had no one to ask after. "So, did Danny tell you why I asked you to come back?"

"Some of it, but I'm sure there's more you can tell me."

Skitch opened a carved box on his desk and offered Jones and Danny a cigarette then took one for himself. He lit them with a monogrammed gold Zippo. Some days, it was good to be the king.

"Something happened about three months ago — didn't seem like much at the time, but I figure that's when it started..."

Janos Bronski and his wife Maria owned a small neighborhood grocery store in West Brownsville where the railroad tracks ran through the middle of the main street parallel to the river. The pair emigrated from Poland just after the war and were trying to make the American Dream work for them. Sam's wife was a little quicker than he at languages, and could talk to the ethnic neighborhood mix in Italian, Slovak, German, Russian, and of course, English.

Their store fronted the river side of the street, nestled between two tenements, the grocery on the first floor, and their living quarters upstairs. The storefront window with Bronski Grocery painted in four-inch letters was Maria's particular pride. Every morning she washed the dust and coke oven soot from it, and anyone passing by could see through the polished glass the neat shelves and counters of an American business.

Besides the stock of canned goods, the store featured generous bins of produce and in one section, herbs and roots that were common remedies for any number of complaints. Everything about the store radiated pride in ownership, and belief in the promise of America.

The man who came in the store wasn't dressed like the workers who lived in the neighborhood. He wore a shiny blue suit and a hand painted necktie; a wide-brimmed hat drooped to his eyebrows. Maria thought he was handsome in a dark, Valentino sort of way, but like so many men who came home from the war, he had a scar. It ran in an angry pink line along his jaw. He came into the store, smiling, pleasant, and asked for a Coca-Cola. Janos was on the step stool stocking the upper shelves with canned goods, so Maria waited on him.

She fetched one from the big red cooler. She handed him the bottle, not sure whether to open it; maybe he wanted to take it with him to drink it later. He handed her a nickel. "*Dzięki*," he said with a nod.

Outside, a train rumbled through, fifty cars of coke and coal bisected the street long ways. "*Masz ładne miejsce tutaj. Musisz być dumni*," he said over the rattle and clank of the hopper cars: You have a nice place here. You must be very proud. Maria smiled and nodded, blushing at the compliment and delighted to hear her native language for a change.

"Did you know," the man said in English, "that there are twenty-two ridges on a bottle cap? Details are important." He held the bottle in his left hand and closed his thumb and forefinger over the neck. He twisted his wrist and with his right thumb, prised the cap from the bottle, bending the cap almost in half. The bottle let off a faint carbonated hiss and a mist rose in the green glass neck.

The man tipped back the bottle and drank it in one draught then handed Maria the bottle in one hand and the folded metal cap in her other. She stared at the cap as if it were a coin a magician had pulled from the air.

He smiled again, pulling his thin moustache into a straight line, and said, "*Bądź bezpieczny.*" Be safe. He stepped onto the sidewalk and strolled past the shop window just as the train's caboose passed by.

Across the street, Maria saw a car. She didn't know the English word "perpendicular," but she could see that the dark green sedan, was aimed at the front of the store from an intersecting street, and moving fast. She screamed and jumped to the side as the car bounced over the curb and crashed through the storefront in a spray of glass, splintering the counter and smashing bins of produce.

The front bumper hit the step stool and sent Janos crashing onto the hood. Maria remembered that the man who jumped out of the car wore a suit, too, but he climbed over the back fender and was out in the street before she could see his face. In a second, he was gone, leaving the sedan sticking half into the street.

"Was either of them hurt?" Jones said, stubbing out his cigarette in the ashtray on Skitch's desk.

Skitch shook his head. "Not much. The husband got a broken arm when he fell on the car. She got a few bumps and bruises."

"You don't think it was an accident?"

Skitch's shoulders rose in a shrug. "The car was stolen from a parking lot outside a bar in Coal Center an hour before. There was a half empty whiskey bottle on the front seat. The car's owner was in the bar passed out when all this went down. It looks like some drunk stole the car and had an accident with it. At least that's how the cops wrote it up."

"Do the Bronskis write numbers for you?" Jones knew that many of the local store owners collected bets for the "policy" game.

"No. Artie Manchin has that neighborhood—the dry cleaner up the street."

"So at least on the surface it wasn't an attack on your operation. You think it was some kind of shakedown? Somebody starting up his own protection game?"

"Nobody asked for money before or after it happened. These were none of my people." He lit another cigarette. "The men were strangers, and nobody's seen them since. Trouble is, it rocked the boat. This is a small town, and it's our town. It runs pretty smooth for us, for the cops, for everybody. People here know they can walk down the street and they won't get mugged, raped, murdered. There's always been an unspoken understanding that nobody touches the women in this town; nobody touches the children; nobody touches the old people. And it's not because the bad guys are afraid of the cops. They're afraid of what we'll do to keep order. As long as things are running on an even keel, the cops just walk their beats and have it easy. The less they have to fight against, the better, and they give us a lot of slack."

"And the grocery store incident changed all that?"

"Not right away, but other things have happened since. A couple of days later, a fight broke out at the Red Feather. Some out-of-towners came in around closing time and started a brawl with the regulars and wrecked the place."

"Anybody killed?"

Skitch shook his head. "No guns or knives. It was all fists and feet."

"And not connected to your operation?"

"Nope. They didn't take money out of the register or even so much as a bottle of hooch, just broke everything they could break and left before the cops arrived."

"Strangers again."

"Nobody recognized any of them."

"And I'm guessing there's more."

"Let me tell you what happened to Tony Rocco..."

VI

Saturday was always a busy day at the Second National Bank. Miners banking their pay filled the drawers with cash, and Martin DeWitt, the bank's president, had an extra off-duty cop inside the bank's entrance. At a quarter to noon, the revolving door spun and one of its wings delivered a hand grenade that slid across the marble floor like a hockey puck.

The grenade went off, but it was all flash and noise; it didn't hurt anyone, but it stunned everybody in the place for a minute. As soon as it went off, a second grenade spun through the door spewing yellow smoke. In seconds, a man in a grey pinstriped suit with a red kerchief over his face ran across the lobby, vaulted the counter, and began stuffing money in a pillow case. One of the tellers tried to stop him and got a pistol across his nose for his trouble.

As the robber ran for the door, the off-duty cop fired at him, missed in the smoke and confusion, and nailed one of the customers. The crook ran through the revolving door and as he hit the sidewalk, grabbed a piece of two-by-four he'd left outside on his way in and threw it between two of the leaves, jamming the door.

The alarm bell was clanging; one of the tellers had the presence of mind to push the button, and plenty of people on the street were watching as the thief ran up the block and climbed into a '37 Nash roadster and sped away, his license plate in full view.

The car was registered to one of Skitch's bag men, Tony Rocco, who lived in a second floor apartment over Moskowitz's Sweeper Repair, and half an hour after the robbery, nine of the Brownsville Police kicked in his door. They found Rocco wound in the arms of his sweetheart, Marcene Bailey, but no red kerchief, no grenades, and no money.

They did find a grey pinstriped suit tossed over a chair in the bedroom, but eye witnesses later said it wasn't the same one. One of them, Mario Lucente, the owner of Lucente's Menswear on Water Street said, "I sell Tony Rocco his clothes, I know my merchandise, and I didn't sell him that cheap-ass suit."

"The cops locked Tony up, sweated him 'til I could get him sprung, and finally had to admit they didn't have evidence to hold him."

"A pretty complicated frame," Jones said.

"It was a work of art," Dodie broke in. "Somebody knew Rocco would be busy at the right time, took his car, wore a suit that looked like one of

... a hand grenade that slid across the marble floor...

his then robbed Second National and let half the town see his license number as he drove away. It was poetry."

"And the customer who was shot?"

"He's okay now."

"No line on the robber?"

Skitch said, "Nope, not the cops, and not us, either. We've had a pretty good truce with them for a while, but this stuff is shaking things up. The robbery investigation's pulling in the State Police and the FBI, and all of a sudden, the locals are all about law enforcement."

"How can I help you?"

"Muscle, I got. It's your brains I need, Jones. I can't figure these guys out. I've had people try to move in, to take over the show before, but it was always head-on. I'm not even sure that's what they want. These bastards strike and disappear before we know what hit us."

"Like Commandos."

Skitch blinked."Huh?"

"Just thinking out loud. What do the Big Boys say?"

"Freddie Greco came down from New Kensington to see me a week ago. The word from the Family is, 'Clean up your house.' I haven't asked for help up to now because I can't afford to look weak. Besides that, it's a matter of pride; we've always handled our own problems here. But word gets around, and we look like pushovers, it reflects on the big operation. If we don't solve this on our own, they'll solve it for us and we'll be out."

"This is all too coordinated to be some local yahoos playing gangster."

"I agree. One thing puzzles me, though; why us?"

"Maybe it's all about location. You've got Route 40 running from one end of the County East to West and the Mon River North to South. They can hit you here and be in West Virginia in twenty minutes, Maryland in thirty, and Ohio in an hour. Maybe Fayette County's just the start of a bigger plan."

"That's where you come in, Jones. You're the detective. Maybe you can figure it out. Are you in?"

"I haven't forgotten who got the Benaducci clan off my back, Skitch. Yeah, I'm in."

Skitch opened a desk drawer and took out a bundle of hundred dollar bills. He counted out five and pushed them across the desk. "This should keep you for a while. Hayes will work with you." Danny nodded in agreement. "Figure this out, Jones, and stop it. I'm counting on you."

#

Neither Danny nor Jones spoke as they rode the elevator to the second floor. When they got off the elevator, another pair of fighters was sparring in the ring, but nobody was paying particular attention.

"Time to start thinking like a detective," Jones said. "Any new people in the outfit? Say, in the last three or four months?"

Danny shook his head. "No, just the regulars."

"How about the gym?"

"People come and go. I'll ask Bucky. He keeps the roster and the locker list. You think this is some kind of inside job? Somebody getting ambitious?"

"I'm thinking in terms of maybe intelligence, infiltration." Jones crossed the floor to the tall windows and looked down to the street. "Hard to tell at this point. I'm just looking at what may have changed before this situation started, if it really is a situation and not a bunch of unrelated coincidences."

"You don't really believe it's a coincidence, do you?"

"Not up front, but I have to look at that as hard as any other possibility until I can rule it out. If these incidents are related, somebody's gone a long way to make them look as if they aren't. Two things bother me right now; the military ordnance and the guy speaking Polish."

"The grenades? Probably some guy's war souvenirs. I recall you pulling one out once."

Jones smiled grimly at the memory. "But not a stun grenade. That's not every day G. I. equipment. You gotta wonder where he got it. We need to check on break-ins at the National Guard armories. Or maybe somebody's selling military ordnance on the sly."

"Okay, I see that, but what about the guy speaking Polish?"

"Is he from the Old Country, or did he learn Polish in the war? The Army didn't teach fluent Polish to rank and file infantrymen. I need to talk to Mrs. Bronski." They started down the stairs to the pool room. "Get the member list for the gym from Bucky. I'll be back in a little while."

"You know where you're going?"

"I'll find it."

Jones crossed the bridge into West Brownsville and sat for ten minutes behind a bus and two cars as a train rumbled down the middle of the main street. Jones timed the cars with the second hand of his watch and did a quick calculation in his head. Five miles an hour, more or less. The caboose passed the crossing, and the striped safety arm rose from the road. The bus and one of the cars in front of him went straight through and up Route 88, while the other car, like Jones, made a right turn and followed the train.

Rows of duplex company houses lined both sides of the street for the first hundred yards then gave way to individual buildings, mostly tenements and shops. Bronski's Grocery was easy to spot. Whitewashed planks were nailed across the store front, and an interior door from a closet or a bedroom hung in a makeshift doorway. Across the top board, Jones read in neat, black letters: "Bronski Grocery" and "Open for Business."

He pulled the Ford to the curb and stepped onto the sidewalk. The street was all but empty. The children were in school this time of the day, and the chill drizzle that fell down Jones's collar kept the casual strollers indoors.

Across the street from the store front was an intersection that opened from the land side of the street. The car that hit the store would have been traveling at least thirty miles per hour to do the damage it did, and would have had to jog about thirty degrees from the intersection. There were no tire marks on the brick street or the sidewalk; they would still have been there had the driver hit his brakes.

Finally, the area away from the side walls wasn't more than a foot clear of the width of a car, left or right. If the driver had missed the window and door area, he would have hit a retaining wall and probably gone through the windshield. Either the driver was a very lucky drunk or a very sober professional.

Jones opened the door and the tinkle of a spring bell surprised him. As soon as Jones stepped inside the store, he felt the itch of his tattoos, runes and wards the OSS had inked into his skin to protect him from the dark magic his Nazi counterparts employed. The tattoos warmed in the presence of magic, and warned Jones of its presence.

The inside of the store was dim because of the boarded window, but as he looked around him, Jones saw evidence of people who didn't give up easily. A broad plank across two sawhorses replaced the smashed counter, and broken bins were cobbled together with scraps of wood. The store was neat and orderly in spite of the "accident." Jones sniffed the air and somewhere, under the odor of cold meat and the earthy smell of potatoes and beets lay a bitter scent of smoldering herbs. Incense.

A stout woman, her dark hair wound in a long braid that encircled her head like a diadem came from the backroom, wiping her hands on her apron, and Jones knew at once that she was the source of the power. "Hello," she said, "can I help you?" with a trace of accent that Jones placed as the region around Krakow.

"*Dzień dobry.*"

Maria Bronski smiled. "*I tobie.*" Her teeth were as straight and perfect as a statue's.

"My name is Jones." He pulled his P.I. folder from his pocket. He flashed is ID and hoped she didn't notice it was from the state of California. "I'm an investigator looking into the accident you had here last month."

Her smile sank into a frown. "That's what the police called it, an accident. You're working for the police?"

"No, I'm not with the police."

"Then why are you here?"

"Certain people see your situation as part of a bigger pattern. Do you think this—" Jones swept an arm around the room—"was an accident?"

Her eyes locked with his. "It was no accident. But I cannot understand why it happened to us. We get along with everyone in the neighborhood. We run an honest business. We bother no one. Why us?"

"Maybe those are the reasons it happened. Maybe whoever did this wanted to frighten not only you but everyone around you; they showed that harm can come to even the least likely people. Tell me about the man who came in before the crash." Jones was careful to avoid the word "accident."

"He was tall, a little taller than you. Dark hair and dark skin. Thin moustache. He wore a suit and a necktie."

"Was he old, young?"

Maria thought a moment. "Thirty years old, maybe. No more."

"Any thing unusual about him?"

"He had a scar." Maria traced a finger along the line of her jaw. "I thought he was a soldier hurt in the war, a — what's the word?"

"A veteran?"

She nodded. "Yes, a veteran."

"And he was very strong." Maria told Jones the story of the bottlecap.

"Do you still have the cap?"

Maria nodded.

"May I see it?"

Maria left for a moment and returned with the bottlecap in her hand. She held it out to Jones in her open palm. When he reached for it, she closed her fingers over his hand, and he felt a charge like electricity course up his forearm. She stared into his eyes and through them into his soul. Jones felt as if something snakelike were slithering around the convolutions of his brain. She let go of his hand and said over her shoulder, "Janos, *wyjść*."

Her husband came from the back room with a rifle to his shoulder, its muzzle pointed at Jones's head. A sling for his broken arm dangled from his neck like a white bandana.

"*On ma zagrożenia.*" Maria told him.

"That's right," said Jones, spreading his arms and turning his hands palm up, "I am no threat."

Janos lowered the muzzle of the rifle but didn't set it down. His eyes studied Jones warily.

"Please forgive our caution, Mister Jones. Since this incident, we have been very careful about strangers."

"No apology necessary." He turned to Janos. "I am here to help."

Janos hesitated for a moment then nodded and set the rifle on the makeshift counter. He slid his arm back into its empty sling.

"About the man who spoke with you, did he ask for money?"

Maria shook her head.

"Did he make any threats?"

"No threats. All he said was, 'Be safe.'"

"And he spoke Polish."

Maria nodded her head. "Yes, he spoke it very well."

"Did he speak as if he were Polish born?"

Maria's eyes drifted slantwise as she weighed her response. "His language seemed too—" She struggled for the right word. "Clean," she said, "with no way I could tell where he was from."

"No accent. And you haven't seen either of these men since?"

Again she shook her head. "No."

Jones looked again at the halved bottle cap in her palm. "May I take that with me?"

Her hand closed over it. "No, Mister Jones. I believe that it will help justice be served someday." Her blue eyes stared into his. "We understand each other, do we not?"

Jones felt a cold finger run down his spine at the icy menace of her words and her tone. "Yes. I believe that we do." He realized that whoever had done this damage had chosen the wrong people to harm, and that their punishment may have little to do with him.

"If we see these creatures again, how may we tell you?"

Jones pulled a small notebook from his pocket and scribbled the number of the pool room on it. He tore out the leaf and handed it to her." You can reach me there. If I'm not in, someone will give me the message." He hesitated and added, "If you feel that you need protection…"

Maria held up her hand in a halting gesture. "Mister Jones, Janos and I survived the Nazi occupation of our country. These men are," her head turned to the side as she sought the correct word, "amateurs." She put the slip of paper into the pocket of her apron. "Thank you for coming, Mister Jones. Perhaps we can help each other. *Do widzenia.*"

"*Do widzenia.*" Jones nodded his head in farewell and left the store more puzzled than he was when he went in. Maria Bronski had powers; was that why she and her husband were singled out? Or were they singled out at all? Was the whole incident random? The case was becoming more tangled by the hour.

#

aria's look into his mind was something he'd experienced before from his MI-5 contact and paramour Deanna Drake, but when she entered his mind, the force was gentle, sharing. Maria's invasion was blunt, almost brutal, shoving his thoughts and defenses aside to get at what she wanted to know.

As he drove across the bridge, Jones decided that he was glad that Maria Bronski was no adversary and planned to do all that he could to keep it that way.

When he got back to the pool room, Danny was waiting for him. "I got the list from Bucky, if you can read it. In the last three months, fourteen new people paid by the week to use the gym. The rest just pay day to day when they show up." He handed Jones the sheet of paper.

"How many are still here?"

"Eight. I put a star by their names."

"How many of them do you know?"

"Ed Donesec, Paul Smith, Mikey Torreo; they're all local guys, and of course, Billy French and Red Jefferson, the boys Fats Mungo brought in. What do you think? One of the newbies is a spy?"

"It's possible. This is the seat of the operation. But just because you know a guy doesn't mean he isn't working for somebody else on the sly. I'd say we need to check on the ones you don't know first, but we can keep an eye on the others in the meantime. I have an errand to run. In the meantime,

I want you to arrange for us to be here after everything closes up tonight. I want to take a look in the lockers."

"I'll tell Dodie."

Jones left his car parked on Snowden Square and walked the three blocks to the Second National Bank building on High Street. It was a medium-sized building as banks go, with a half-pillared granite façade over brick. Jones chuckled as he went through the revolving door at the thought of the bank guards stymied by a two-by-four.

The bank's interior was testimony to more prosperous times: plenty of marble, brass, and polished oak. The tellers' windows were arranged in a half moon around the entrance to the vault. Of the twelve, Jones counted tellers at six in the middle of a workday, a sign that business was slackening.

He waited in one of the lines while an elderly woman counted out a pile of coins. Next a businessman pulled a drawstring bank bag from his coat and laid out his day's receipts for the teller to sort. When it was his turn, the teller, a petite brunette in a round-collared blouse gave him her hundredth smile of the day, and to her credit, it looked genuine.

"Good afternoon, sir. How may I help you?"

"I need a cashier's check. Can you do that from this window?"

"Certainly. There is a two-dollar fee for issuing a cashier's check. What is the amount?"

"Five hundred dollars."

She nodded and held her smile. "For amounts over fifty dollars, we must have the cash in hand before we write the check."

Jones nodded and returned her smile. "Can't be too careful." He took his bankroll from his pocket and her eyes widened as Jones peeled off five one hundred dollar bills and two singles. He fanned them and laid them on the counter.

The teller's smile had become frozen. She picked up the bills and said, "Just one moment, please." She turned away and took the bills to a man at a desk near the vault entrance. She leaned in and spoke quietly to him, gesturing toward Jones with her shoulder. He looked at each bill in its turn, through the lenses of his glasses and then over their rims with his naked eye. Finally satisfied that they weren't counterfeit, he nodded his head and she left his desk.

The teller returned and said, "If you will please write down the name of the payee, I can have your check issued immediately." She pushed a slip of paper across the counter to him. Jones kept his hands at his sides. They were already suspicious of him. He wasn't going to leave any fingerprints. If the Feds wanted to find him, they would, but why make it easy for them?

"The payee's name is Isaac Jacobs." He didn't pick up the pen, and for an uncomfortable moment, neither he nor the teller moved. Her smile faded. Then, looking over his shoulder at the people queuing up behind him, she picked up the pen. Jones spelled the last name for her, and in two minutes, she returned with the printed check. "Will there be anything else?"

"Yeah," Jones said, laying three singles on the counter. Could you please change that for me? Quarters will do." Jones dropped the coins in his pocket and walked out through the revolving door.

He found a phone booth around the corner and sidled in, shutting the door behind him. He dialed for the operator, and she came on the line almost immediately. "I'd like to place a person-to-person call."

"To what city?"

"Los Angeles, California." Jones gave her the number.

"The party's name?"

"Isaac Jacobs."

"One moment, please."

Jones listened to the hum and click of the terminals and the phone began to ring in California. One ring, two, three, with a rain barrel echo to them.

"Hello."

"Person-to-person telephone call for Isaac Jacobs."

"That's me," the gruff voice said.

"Go ahead, sir."

Jones waited a three count to make sure the operator was off the line. "Isaac, it's me." Jones didn't use his name.

"Glad you called." Isaac Jacobs, blind since Guadalcanal, knew people by voices better than most did by sight. "Line's clear." He could also detect subtle changes in the sound, indicating a tap or multiple parties listening in. "You got more calls since you left town than you did while you was here."

"Anybody I know?"

"Most of them didn't leave names. One dumb sumbitch called me three times the same day, give three different names and three different callback numbers, as if I couldn't recognize his voice. Fourth time he called, I said, 'Look, Mister Smith, Johnson, Tyler, or whatever the hell name you're using this round, why you playing games with a poor blind black man?'" Isaac cackled. "He hung up and didn't call again."

"Good work. Listen, Isaac, you'll get a letter in a few days. Don't open it in front of anybody."

"You got my box number?"

Jones knew it but said instead, "Five-C," code for the amount so that Isaac wouldn't be cheated by an unscrupulous teller.

"Bingo."

"I'll call again in a few days. Be careful, Isaac."

"No need. I ain't the one folks're shooting at." Isaac hung up.

IX

Jones needed a place to sleep, so he went looking. The last time he was in Brownsville, he'd stayed at the Brownsville Hotel, but a shootout on the fire escape that left two dead bodies and a lot of holes in the plaster pretty much guaranteed that he wouldn't be welcome there again.

Along Water Street below the Pennsy roundhouse, he found a brick tenement with a tavern on the ground floor. A sign over the side door read: Rooms by the Week. A ten-dollar bill bought him two weeks' worth of a bed he could sleep in and a door he could close. The building manager, a cross-eyed runt with a two-day stubble on his cheeks handed him a key and a set of sheets.

Jones remembered that the place catered to the railroad workers, which was okay with him. They worked long hours at odd shifts, came home tired, and wouldn't pay any attention to his coming and going.

The second floor room was eerily reminiscent of his flop in L.A.: a bare floor, a lumpy single bed, a beat-up chest of drawers, an empty doorless closet and one chair. Through the runny glass of the window, Jones saw a narrow alley two floors below with grass growing between the bricks and a line of garbage cans like soldiers on review. No fire escape. It would do. He put his duffel on the bed and walked out, locking the door behind him.

One more piece of business before he went back to Snowden Square; Jones stepped into a phone booth on the corner and dialed a number from memory. Three rings and a man's nasal voice answered. "Yeah?"

"Coakee?"

"Who's asking?"

"C.O. Jones."

"I'll be....go to hell. We all thought you were dead."

"Someday, but not this week."

"Still driving the '41 Super Deluxe I set up for you?"

"Yeah, that's why I called. It could use a tune up and a few holes patched."

Coakee laughed. "What caliber?"

"Thirty, as a matter of fact. It needs some windows replaced too."

"Bring her on up. You remember the way?"

"I'll find you. Sometime tomorrow."

"See you then."

Earl Coakee, master mechanic, adapted cars for the Lytle Brothers' moonshine operation. He did the setup for the Ford coupe that had served Jones so well. Coakee's rickety old barn in the middle of a mountain forest housed a machine shop that would do General Motors proud. He was the closest thing to a magician the mechanical world could produce.

Jones would likely have to leave the car for a day or two, but Coakee would loan him one in the meantime. Now to get back to business.

X

anny was waiting for him, sitting on a sidewalk bench across the street from the pool room. He was reading the newspaper, a cigarette dangling from the corner of his mouth. "So, Jonesey, who do you think will win the big one, Ezzard Charles or Pat Valentino?"

"My money's on Charles. Anybody who can dust Jersey Joe Walcott's got the stuff."

Danny nodded, agreeing. "You know his manager Tom Tannas is from around here; not exactly local, from Arnold."

"Up beside New Kensington, right?"

"Yep."

There's that town again, thought Jones, a town so connected it was known generally as "Little Chicago," the seat of power where Skitch got his marching orders. "Anything else big in the news?"

Danny turned the paper back to the front page to show the headline: U.S. Communist Party Leaders Convicted of Sedition. "Found fourteen of them guilty. I hope they hang 'em all. I didn't fight for four years to have a bunch of Reds move in and take over the country."

Scapegoats, Jones thought, for what was really going wrong in the U.S., and for that matter, the world. "So are we set for tonight?" Jones said, changing the subject.

"Yeah. We can stick around at closing time. I looked the lockers over. Most of them have just the gym's lock on them. Bucky gave me the spare keys. A few have padlocks besides."

"I'll take care of those."

"I figured you could. You know, Jones, I don't know what you did in the war, but somebody did one hell of a job training you for it."

"Mostly, I paid attention. That's how you learn. I don't know about you, but my stomach's growling. Come on, I'll buy you a steak."

Moe's was a train-car diner that specialized in two things: steak and eggs. Most days the eggs were tougher than the steak, but the price was right. The place was half empty; it would fill up soon when the shifts changed and the working stiffs came in hungry. They took stools at the end of the counter. Grease crackled and popped on the broad iron griddle, and a thin haze of smoke blued the air.

"Wanna see a menu?" Danny said with a laugh as Moe came over. Moe was about five feet even and as wide as a door, but his stomach was flat. He wore a white apron dotted with the day's grease over a T-shirt and an olive green garrison cap with an Infantry medallion left front. His florid face and gin blossom nose testified to a lifelong love affair with the bottle.

Danny stood and saluted. "What's with the hat, Moe?"

"Goddamn Board of Health come in here last week. Said I had to either wear a hat or a snood to keep from getting hair in the food. As if that's a hazard." He pulled off the cap revealing a shining bald crown. "And as if any of my customers gave a damn." He jammed the cap back on his head. "Whattaya want?"

"I'd order the chicken a la king blue plate special, but it always gives me heartburn. How about steak and eggs?"

"Steak and eggs I got." He turned to Jones. "You?"

"The same."

"You got it." Moe turned away and trundled over to the griddle.

"Moe landed at D-Day," Danny said. "He's got some stories that'll make your hair stand on end, but if you want to hear them, you have to catch him when he's plastered."

"I guess everybody who went over does."

"How about you, Jonesey? I bet you've got a few."

Jones turned to look Danny in the eye. "Some stories are better left untold," he said. His tone and the look on his face dampened the mood, and Danny shut up.

XI

PARIS 3 April 1944

The brick streets were glazed with a chilly rain that still fell in fits and bursts. Lieutenant Simmons, code name Wormwood, huddled in a doorway off the *Rue des Pauvres*. He wanted a cigarette but couldn't risk the flare of a match or the glowing tip giving him away. From his covert, he could see the only apparent entrance to the target building, No.324. His counterpart Walter Bennet, code name Cyclops, watched from a parallel street.

Twice since nightfall, German troops rode through on patrol in their Volkswagen "tub cars" shining spotlights and aiming rifles in dark corners and alleys. Each time, Simmons turned his hooded face to the wall and the beam danced over him. His wards didn't make him invisible, but they seemed to amplify the darkness around him.

In the distance, the famous clock on the facade of the *Palais de Justice* across the Seine chimed two a.m. For some reason, the occupying Nazis spared it when they took the city; maybe it appealed to their sense of order. The temperature was falling, and Simmons was beginning to think that nothing would happen that night, just as nothing had happened the night before.

Sources in the Resistance had told of the house and its sinister reputation, of its links to the worship of things born before Satan had ever thought of rebellion. A place of darkness in the City of Light. People came to the brooding black mansion nestled between more modern houses like a mysterious old book between newer brighter volumes. People came, and sometimes never left. Superstitious locals called it *"le Bouche d'Enfer,"* the Mouth of the Inferno, or more colloquially, the Mouth of Hell.

Simmons had once seen the silent movie *Metropolis*, and No. 324 reminded him of the mad scientist Rotwang's house, not so much its overall appearance, for its façade had no feature but a doorway—no windows—but its incongruity, a blackened medieval eyesore nestled among the bright and modern buildings on the street.

"Ralph Adams Cram knew of the place, was even in it once," Colonel Hennessey had told them in the briefing. "He changed names and disguised the address and some details about the location, but there is no mistaking; it is the same locus of power." Hennessey handed each of them a slim bound volume. "This is Cram's book, *Black Spirits and White*. The first story 'No. 252 Rue M. le Prince' gives a good description of the place. Read it carefully; Cram was an architect and he paid close attention to detail. I would have preferred to consult him directly, but he died two years ago."

"I've heard of him," Cyclops said. "He was pretty famous wasn't he?"

Hennessey nodded. "He was *Time Magazine's* Man of the Year for 1926. But so was Adolf Hitler for 1938. Cram was a student of classical architecture and distinguished himself by designing a number of impressive cathedrals."

"Just curious," Simmons said. "Do any of them have 'properties?'" the Outfit's code word for occult powers.

Hennessey coughed. "That information, gentlemen, is classified. When the Nazis marched into Paris, we knew that one of their objectives was to take possession of the house. It occupies a sort of crossroads of paths of power, *Heilige Linien' to* the Germans 'Fairy Paths' to the Irish, 'Dragon Lines' to the Chinese."

"Ley Lines said Cyclops.

"Yes, Ley Lines." Hennessey went on. "Where they intersect, they amplify each other.

Our sources tell us that for a short time, trucks under heavy guard would deliver crates and boxes to the place. That activity has slowed for the moment, but what they are doing there is apparently not complete."

"What is going on there?" Cyclops said.

"They seem to be assembling something, gathering the right combination of elements, possibly to tap into the power the place holds."

"Why wasn't the place torn down years ago, if it's so dangerous?" Simmons asked.

"At first, the French thought the place may be useful, but the more they learned about it, the more reluctant they became to tamper with an unknown quantity that is so potentially dangerous. It has been a case of 'let sleeping dogs lie.'"

"Or maybe sleeping dragons." Cyclops added.

"And there is another curiosity. For two months, the Nazis have been methodically looting the catacombs under the city, collecting bones under the supervision of these men." Hennessey slid two photographs across the table.

"Who are they?"

"The man in the SS uniform is Albert Stengler, a top shelf operative in the SS occult unit. The civilian is a collaborator named Duval Chirac." The photo of Chirac showed a short, balding man with thyroidal eyes and a prominent chin.

"The Nazis have been collecting bones under the supervision of these men."

Cyclops looked up from the photos. "You said they're gathering bones."

"Gathering isn't exactly the word; perhaps selecting is more accurate. These two take a team into the catacombs and will have them dislodge a mass of bones then Chirac will pick through them for hours, measuring them, weighing them, gauging them by criteria we can only imagine. He may spend three hours and come away with no more than a half dozen at a time."

"It seems like a tedious job," Simmons said. "There are what—six million people's remains down there. Is this Chirac a sorcerer?"

Hennessey shook his head. "No, he's not a magician. Chirac is a sculptor. We believe the Nazis have either completed or nearly completed building this."

Hennessey unrolled a photostatic copy and weighed its curling edges down with a coffee cup and an ashtray. The words "top secret" were stamped in one corner in red. "It is Ο Συλλέκτης , literally translated from the Greek, 'The Gatherer.'" He pronounced it "O sylléktis."

Simmons stared at the photostat. It was a copy of an ancient picture ragged around the edges of its parchment. The image was all the more chilling for its white-on-black depiction of what appeared to be an elaborate cone built of human bones. But the bones were not simply piled; they were attached to each other in a ghastly filigree, leaving the interior of the cone hollow. The arrangement of the bones included a number of runic and other symbols, geometric figures, some repeated and others unique. Some were the same symbols tattooed on Simmons' torso. Inside the cone a throne-like seat made of femurs was placed at the center, the top of its backrest capped with a line of skulls. Based on scale, the cone had to be at least twenty feet tall at its apex. The design looked to Simmons like Indian teepees he'd seen in books with totemic symbols painted on them.

"This is probably a dumb question," said Cyclops after a pause. "What does it gather?"

Hennessey stared at the picture. "It gathers power."

"You said the name was Greek." Simmons said. "Is that the origin of the Gatherer?"

"From what we can deduce, it predates ancient Greek civilization. Its origin is a mystery, but similar designs have been found in Mayan ruins and in one Egyptian scroll."

"But never the actual — what would you call it? A device?"

"Yes. Device is a good word, although it has no moving parts like a piece of machinery."

"If it works, why hasn't one been found?"

"Because it is too dangerous, a wild card." Hennessey produced another photograph, this one of workmen in coveralls attaching bones to a similar structure. The cone was approximately two thirds complete. "We have never found any source of information as to controlling a *Sylléktis*. We attempted to build one, as you see in that photograph, but before it was complete, the energy fields it gave off were so disruptive that we had to dismantle it."

"And you believe the Nazis have found the key to controlling it?"

"That is our fear. And that is why Chirac must be stopped, and be stopped before 30 April."

"*Walpurgisnacht.*"

"Precisely. Cram's story tells of a reputed conclave in the house every year on that date. If the Germans control *O Sylléktis* on a night when the barriers between our world and the other is the weakest, the consequences could be unimaginable."

"Okay," Cyclops broke in. "Stengler is in charge of gathering bones, and Chirac is in charge of putting them together, but who's in charge of running the device?"

"That is an unknown factor," Hennessey replied, "But it would take an accomplished sorcerer to employ *O Sylléktis*."

"And do we bring back souvenirs?" The Outfit's code for captured relics.

Hennessey shook his head. "No souvenirs. The mission is search and destroy. Absolutely."

XII

"Hey Jonesey, your steak's getting cold." Danny pulled Jones from his reverie.

"Yeah, right." He picked up his knife and fork and began sawing at the steak.

"I thought you were right-handed."

A bite stopped halfway to Jones's mouth. He was holding his fork in his left hand. "I am, but it never hurts to teach yourself to do everything with both." Jones was not naturally ambidextrous; it was an acquired skill as part of his training for espionage.

"Can you wank with your left hand, boy?" Major Fitzpatrick, his instructor at Camp X had asked him. "How about wiping your arse?" The questions startled the young Lieutenant Simmons. "You want to convince the Krauts that you're a left-handed German, you have to go full kettle. They catch you doing the least little thing with your right hand, it's Sweet Fanny Adams, lad."

"You're right-handed, Danny," said Jones. "What if you broke it? How well would you do with your secondary hand? We're in a rough business. How fast could you pull and fire with your left? And how well could you aim? Something to think about."

"You're right, Jonesey," Danny said around a bite of steak. "I'll have to practice with my left hand. Who knows; it might save my life some day."

"All that does is postpone the inevitable, Danny. 'Time and chance happeneth to them all.'"

"Where's that from?"

"Ecclesiastes 9:11."

Danny chuckled. "I never took you for a Bible reader, Jonesey."

"Sometimes it was the only book available."

"I read it too, with Sister Georgina standing over me with a yardstick in grade school."

"And look where we ended up anyway."

XIII

"I don't get it," Cyclops said. "If this is such a top secret big deal, why does everybody come and go through the front door?"

The afternoon sun shone through the gap in the curtains and painted a golden rectangle on the far wall of the flat.

"I don't know. According to the Resistance, there are no underground passages or entrances leading into the mansion, at least none that they know."

"Maybe the Jerrys are just cocky; they think because they've held the city for four years that nobody can touch them. They don't even have guards posted outside No. 324."

"That's what worries me more than anything," Simmons said. "If they don't have sentries outside, what do they have guarding the place on the inside?"

A knock at the door, three quick, two slow, three quick. Cyclops drew his pistol and stood to the side of the door. "*Oui?*"

An envelope slid under the door. Cyclops waited until the footsteps retreated down the hallway before stooping to retrieve it. He held it in his hand and closed his eyes. "It is from de Lancre, delivered by one of his people." He tore it open and found a single piece of paper, a diagram. "It's a sketch of the building next door." He handed the drawing to Simmons. "They've found a passage through the walls from the cellar of the house next door into No. 324. It's concealed now, but maybe we can break through and get into the other house from below."

Simmons' eyes strayed to the trunk across the room. "If we can't get into it, do we have enough ordnance to take down both buildings?"

"If we set it right, sure we do."

"Tomorrow, then."

Cyclops nodded agreement. "Tomorrow."

Cyclops' special talent was his ability to read the history of an object based on who had touched it and how recently. He described the sensation as looking at a queue of people receding into the distance; the first was the sharpest, and each predecessor more vague than the last until the faces blurred into obscurity. "It's a good thing it works as it does," he once told Simmons. "If I saw only the last person something touched, I'd handle a dagger and see only the corpse it was stuck in."

He studied the diagram. "This may be how Sar Torrevieja, or whatever his real name might have been, got in and out of the place without being seen."

Simmons nodded. If Cram's story is based on a real house and real events, it is also likely that Cram's character was based on a real sorcerer. "The passage is sealed. The Nazis aren't using it, but that doesn't mean they don't know about it. It's not like them to leave no means of escape."

"And Sar Torrevieja?"

"'King of the Sorcerers.' Long dead, I'd imagine. If we take Cram's story as gospel, the man was alive in 1886; that's almost 60 years ago.

Cyclops was silent almost long enough for Simmons to think the subject closed. Then he said, "But you and I both know that wizards live long lives."

The night passed slowly. It was agreed that the operation take place in the daylight hours. The team would be less likely stopped and questioned during the early morning crush of people going to their jobs. For an occupied city, Paris had adapted remarkably well, and life went on day to day despite the heavy hand of the Nazis controlling that life. As for the magic, as Hennessey had once told Simmons, "It is like the wind or electricity; it is neither good nor evil. It simply exists, and like the laws of physics, as we discover them, the rules of magic become a means to an end." And like electricity or the wind, the force of magic needed neither daylight nor darkness to function.

The dead time before an operation used to gnaw at Simmons, but years in the field had grown a thick callus over the anxiety a pending mission brought. Cyclops sharpened his Ka-Bar again, cleaned his pistol, although he did so the day before and the day before that; unloaded the clip and reloaded it, examining each round. Simmons made no comment. Every man had his own ritual. Each reacted in his own way to the thought that living another day depended largely on luck and his own resources. While Cyclops exhausted his nervous energy, Simmons sat in a chair by the window and read "No. 252 Rue M. le Prince" for the third time.

"The way Cram tells it, the first two floors are ordinary; it's the third level of the place that's odd. But if the *Sylléktis* is built to scale, none of the rooms on any of the floors could accommodate its height, even the round room with the pentagram in the floor and the dome in the ceiling, if it exists."

"The Colonel seems to think the depiction's accurate, and I don't doubt him. He always holds more cards than we see. But you're right; based on the dimensions of the place, there is no ceiling high enough for the device to stand."

"I guess we'll find out soon enough."

"If we live long enough." Cyclops went back to sharpening his knife.

The plan was simple, and relied on the Resistance's knowledge of the tunnels and subterranean canals that comprised the Parisian sewer system. Their liaisons, Jacques De Lancre and Axel Peret would lead them through the underground maze and evade the Nazi patrols to enter the house next door to No. 324.

De Lancre arrived alone an hour before dawn. He was clean shaven the day before, but now he sported a thick moustache that curved almost to his chin. "Where is Axel?" Simmons said.

Jacques hung his head. "He was taken yesterday. The Nazi soldiers broke down his door and arrested him, his father, and his brother."

"Will it compromise the mission?" Cyclops asked.

Jacques' head snapped up and his eyes blazed for a second at what seemed a callous question then sadness returned to his face. "No, my friend, it will not. His family knew nothing of our plans, and Axel would die before he revealed anything to the *Boches*. We will succeed. We three simply will have to do the work of four."

Doing the work of four included a redivision of supplies and equipment to conceal it all under the loose fitting canvas coats, baggy trousers and tool bags of workmen that de Lancre provided. The explosives were already hidden near the site, de Lancre assured them. He would lead them there and go no further. It was not that he lacked courage or will; de Lancre lacked the wards the Americans had as protection from whatever magical forces the Nazis might employ in No. 324. Once they entered the mansion, the Americans were on their own.

The weapons they carried would be minimal: handguns and knives in the work clothes' concealed pockets. Detonator wires were hidden inside a coil of rope, and blasting caps in the hollowed handles of work worn hammers. Parts of the detonator were cleverly disguised as tools; the battery lay buried in a tin of grease.

De Lancre gave Simmons and Cyclops forged identity papers that marked them as sewer maintenance personnel. They would cross the city on foot, concealing themselves in plain sight until they entered the underground tunnels four blocks away from the *Rue des Pauvres*. The Americans' French was more than sufficient to pass them off as natives; if they were stopped and questioned, they could deflect suspicion.

So, as the sun rose over the City of Light, the three set off, workmen on their way to a day of hard, dirty labor, in clothes redolent of rot and human waste. "I'd tell you two to stand downwind," Cyclops quipped, "but I smell just as bad as you do."

Simmons hoped that his partner's humor wasn't a mask for underlying fear. Absolute fearlessness sometimes led to complacency. It was sensible to be a little bit afraid in the face of danger; that little bit of fear gave an edge, heightened the perceptions. But if that fear crossed an indefinable line, it opened the door to panic. Simmons had partnered with Cyclops three times before and found him each time to be cool under pressure, but the sun rose new each day.

They passed the *Gare D'Orsay*, the former railway depot converted into a postal center at the outbreak of war. Down the river, through the early morning mist, Simmons saw the spires of the Notre Dame cathedral. He imagined Quasimodo deafened by the bells, another servant damaged by duty, and he wondered what damage he would sustain before his duty was over.

Two German soldiers stood at either side of the pedestrian bridge over the Seine that connected the *Gare D'Orsay* to *les Tuileries*, the grand public gardens and at its extremity, the *Jeu de Paume*, the National Gallery that once displayed Monet's Water Lillies and now warehoused art works confiscated by the Nazis like so many bolts of silk or bales of cotton.

The trio strolled nonchalantly onto the bridge, amid a throng of pedestrians. The soldiers' eyes measured every person who passed them. From the corner of his eye, Simmons saw one of the soldiers nudge another and point in their direction.

"*Vous trois, arrêtez.*"

The four soldiers converged in a rough semi-circle in front of them. The German who had spoken eyed them suspiciously. "Where are you going, and what is your business? His French was better than most.

"We work in the sewers," said de Lancre, gesturing to his crusted rubber boots. The soldier stared coldly at him for a three count as if weighing the truth of his words. He took the Frenchman's tool bag from him and opened it. He looked inside, and his mouth twisted in disgust at the caked waste in the crevices of the tools. He handed the bag back to de Lancre without speaking.

De Lancre turned his palms up in a gesture of innocence. "Besides, my friend, who would wear clothes that smell like these if he didn't have to?"

The soldier snorted and repeated the remark to his companions in German. They all laughed, and their leader turned to Cyclops. "Your bag." He said it in English. To his credit, Cyclops didn't flinch. Instead, he squinted one eye and said, "*Je ne comprends pas.*"

At that moment, an explosion rocked the far corner of *les Tuleries*. Simmons, Chirac and Cyclops were suddenly forgotten as the Nazi troopers dashed across the bridge to the site where smoke was already rising.

Out of earshot, de Lancre said to the Americans, "Our guardian angels are watching closely. Let us go while we can."

While most of the crowd lined the railing of the bridge, the trio resisted the temptation to dash across and stopped to gawk, fitting in with the crowd before moving along at a leisurely pace.

"We have learned that like small children, the Nazis are easily distracted by a bright flash or a loud noise," Chirac said as they left the bridge. "It is easy to make them jump and run like trained dogs. We know that we cannot defeat them head-on, but every day we throw them off balance a little and chip away at the fear they use to keep their hold on our people.

"The Germans have become complacent. They think they own the chair, but they sit in it only for the moment. Like the drip of water that becomes a stream that becomes a river, that carves a canyon through a mountain, we will wear them down and take away their authority."

When the Nazis took Paris, they understood that a city so large, so old, and with so many entrenched institutions vital to its day-to-day operation would have to be either co-opted or destroyed. They saw the inefficiency of reinventing and replacing systems, bureaucracies, and operations and they realized that to disrupt any of them would start Paris down a slippery decline into chaos. So, the occupying Germans eventually settled into an almost business-as usual arrangement for the functions of the city.

A truck chugged by, a third of its bed taken up by an Imbert downdraft generator powered by coal in the absence of ready gasoline. Having no native petroleum sources and all imports stopped, the French adjusted to the situation by using gasification to power their internal combustion engines.

"Amazing how they've adapted to it all," Cyclops said, speaking flawless French.

"They've been here since before the Middle Ages," Simmons replied. "I have a feeling they'll still be here long after the Nazis are gone."

Several blocks beyond the *Tuleries*, they arrived at a sort of trap door made of sheet iron set into the ground a few feet from the pavement. De Lancre tugged at its iron ring. The hinges groaned, and fetid air wafted from the tunnels below. An iron-runged ladder led into the darkness. "Come, my friends," de Lancre said, stepping into the portal. "If you hesitate, our friend on the corner," de Lancre twitched his eyes toward a German soldier waiting to cross the street, "may find us suspicious."

The trio clambered down the ladder, and found themselves in a different world, one of groined and vaulted arches and water that stretched as far as the light of their electric torches could reach.

"'Paris has another Paris under itself,'" Simmons said.

"Ah!" said de Lancre. "You have read Hugo." He continued the quotation, "'A Paris of sewers; which has its streets, its crossings, its squares, its blind alleys, its arteries, and its circulation, which is slime, minus the human form.'"

"Jean Valjean."

"His nemesis Javert reminds me of the agents of the Gestapo. One could only wish that they would all meet the same end, link their arms and walk to the bottom of the Seine." He pointed his light to the right. "This way. You see the line of the high water. It has receded as Spring has come, so our walk will be less difficult."

The water was thigh deep, and cold. As they sloshed through it behind de Lancre, Simmons and Cyclops could hear a constant medley of dripping, gurgling, and the occasional splattering of water from a drain pouring into the dun flow. The sounds echoed through the sewer's emptiness. A cool draft blew through the tunnels, but did little to dampen the smell of the city's waste. Rats scuttled along the walls, finding purchase on the narrowest of ledges.

They turned a corner and saw a stone walkway like a narrow sidewalk that stretched into the darkness. De Lancre climbed out of the water. "We are close now. There were no guards along here yesterday or the day before, but we should take no chances." He doused his torch, and the others followed suit. "One hundred thirty paces and we will arrive."

For Simmons, it was only one hundred nineteen, but his legs were longer than de Lancre's. The Frenchman stood silent for a full minute listening then lit his torch. The beam played along the stones until he found a small mark, an X in white chalk. Simmons could see that the mortar around the mark was a different shade of grey than the rest of the wall.

De Lancre set his bag on the walkway and drew out a hammer and chisel. "Now, my friends, we go to work."

Removing the stones took little time because they had been chiseled out previously and repointed with a weak mix of cement. In moments, a man-sized hole was opened. De Lancre slipped through it and motioned Simmons and Cyclops to follow him. "We are in a subcellar of No. 326, the house to the north of the target. The residents of the house were evicted, as were those of the house on the other side. Yesterday, there were two guards on the ground floor." He turned the beam of his light to a large canvas knapsack in the corner. "There is your ordnance. Bring it and follow me."

Across the cellar a flight of stone stairs followed the curve of the wall. At the top, de Lancre reached upward toward a trap door.

"Wait," Cyclops whispered. "He reached past Chirac and put his palm against the sheet of iron. He closed his eyes for a moment then said. "No one had touched this flap since your man yesterday. Before that, German soldiers, but so long ago, their image is a dim shadow. It is safe."

The trap door swung open on silent hinges oiled the day before and opened into a dust-laden basement cluttered with old furniture, boxes, and rubbish. Dim grey light filtered through two street side windows at the far end. An empty wine rack lay on its side like a dust covered skeleton in a corner.

De Lancre and Cyclops crept into the basement. Simmons waited behind to push the knapsack through the opening. de Lancre gave a hand signal for his companions to wait as he drew a pistol from inside his coat. Even in the dim light, Simmons recognized the distinctive shape of a Luger, likely taken from a dead German, its barrel extended by a silencer. Most of the Resistance firepower came from stolen firearms, and Simmons appreciated the ironic satisfaction of killing the enemy with their own weapons.

De Lancre crossed the basement toward a rickety set of wooden stairs leading upward into the house. Cyclops went first. He touched the knob of the door at the top. He nodded, and de Lancre sidled past him. The Frenchman took an entire minute to turn the knob before opening the door a crack to peer through it. He gave a signal to wait and stole noiselessly through the doorway and into the house beyond.

Simmons could hear a radio playing faint music but could not hear the cat-paw tread of de Lancre's feet as he crept through the ground floor of the house. Then he heard the phut-phut of the silenced Luger and the thud of two bodies on the floor overhead.

Simmons and Cyclops passed through the doorway and found themselves in a pantry off a well-equipped kitchen. They followed a hallway to the front of the house and found de Lancre heaving a dead soldier into a red leather armchair.

He crossed one of the corpse's legs over the other as if he were sitting in a relaxed position then laid the soldier's weapon, a Gehwer carbine, across his lap, curling his right hand around the trigger and his left around the barrel. To anyone looking through the window from the sidewalk into the house's dim interior, he would appear to be on duty, guarding the door.

"Help me," he hissed. They dragged the second guard to the next room out of sight from the street. De Lancre eyed his companions. He nodded to Cyclops. "You will better fit in his uniform." In moments, Cyclops was transformed into a German sentry. "Now," de Lancre said, "the wall."

#

Midnight. The din of the pool room had faded as the shooters left one by one until only Danny and Jones were left, shooting at a table in front of one of the plate glass windows. Bucky came from behind the counter to pull the window shades down then flipped the hanging sign on the glass door from open to "closed."

Skitch and Dodie had left earlier, and the card game upstairs broke up an hour before. The building was empty except for the three of them.

Bucky turned off the overheads and put on his jacket. "You guys make sure you lock the door when you leave, okay, Danny?"

Danny looked up from his shot. The shaded light over the pool table made his straw colored hair glow. "Don't worry, Bucky. We'll take care of it. I'll give back your keys tomorrow morning."

"Yeah." Bucky nodded and hesitated as if he wanted to say something else.

"What is it, Bucky?"

"I think I saw something tonight, something not right."

Danny chalked his cue stick. "Tell us about it, Buck."

"I was swamping out the showers and I come through the locker room with the mop and bucket. I saw one of the new guys, that Mateosky in his locker, only I don't think it was his locker. I think it was the one next to his. He saw me come in and he slammed it shut quick before I could be sure."

Danny unfolded the list Bucky gave him earlier. He showed the list to Jones and pointed to the name. "Dave Mateosky. Locker number sixteen." Then to Bucky, "Did he have anything in his hands, like maybe he stole something?"

Bucky shook his head. "Not that I could see."

"What locker was he in that wasn't his own?" Jones asked.

"Number seventeen, I think. Maybe eighteen, but it was on that side of his."

"Did you say anything to him?"

Bucky looked at the floor. "Uh, no I didn't." His voice trailed off.

"You know this Mateosky, Danny?" Jones said.

"Seen him around. Big dude, about six-five, all muscle, not like a body builder, more like a shaved gorilla. He comes in and works with the barbells. I've seen him bench four hundred pounds."

Jones understood why Bucky didn't challenge Mateosky; he was afraid of him. "That's okay, Bucky," he said. "You did good telling us. You go on now. Just keep a sharp eye out."

Bucky left, closing the street door behind him.

"Locker seventeen, huh?" Danny said.

"Time to go to work."

"One second," Danny replied. "Eight ball right side the hard way."

Danny cued his shot, and the white ball collided with the black eight with a sharp crack. The eight caromed off the rail and zipped across the table, slamming with a thud into the side pocket.

"Nice shot."

Danny grinned. "Now I only owe you eight bucks."

Upstairs the gym was dark and silent. Faint light from the street below shone through the tall windows, casting distorted rectangles on the ceiling. The smell of leather and sweat was augmented by a new odor, hot metal. The radiators along the walls clanked and gurgled.

"I guess Skitch had Bucky fire the boiler tonight," Danny said, turning his head toward the sound.

"'Tis the season."

"You've never been here in the winter, have you, Jonesey?"

"Nope. But I guess it's like winter in plenty of other places I've been."

"You wouldn't think so, but the river freezes a foot thick in February. You can drive a car across it."

"I'll look forward to it."

The locker room lay between the gym and the showers at the rear of the building. The room had no windows, so it was safe to turn on the lights. The locker room was long and narrow, with a bench down the center and ranks of tall olive drab lockers lining the walls.

"Army surplus?" Jones asked.

"I think they fell off a truck on their way to Indiantown Gap."

The floor was a hexagonal checkerboard of black and white tiles that shone in the light from the bare bulbs overhead. The smell of disinfectant and bleach mingled with the odor of dirty socks and old tennis shoes.

There were thirty-six lockers in all, each with a unique key. Danny pulled a jangling wire loop of them from his pocket. Serial numbers for each lock were stamped on the flimsy tin keys, but Bucky had scratched a larger number on the shoulder of each with a nail to make it easier for him to see which key belonged to a given locker.

"Here's Mateosky's locker." Jones toggled the sliding handle and found it locked as he expected. A cheap padlock was threaded through matching rings on the metal door and frame. The brand name, Wahler, was enameled on the smooth sides. The paint was unmarred; the lock was new.

Danny flipped through the keys on the ring. "Thirteen, fourteen, fifteen; here it is."

He held the key to locker sixteen between his thumb and forefinger as he handed the whole ring to Jones. The key fit. Next was the padlock. Jones drew a small leather case from his pocket and selected a pair of shining steel picks. He slid one then the other into the keyhole and worked them side to side, feeling the pins. He frowned.

"Problem?"

"If this lock was a standard Yale, it'd be open already. Sometimes these cheap numbers are harder to open even with the key because the parts aren't machined precisely." He worked a little longer, and the lock clicked. Jones pulled the shackle and it popped open.

Inside the locker, they found the standard uniform for the gym rat, sweats, rubber-soled canvas shoes, dirty white cotton socks, and a wide leather kidney belt for back support. A paper sack lay at the back of the shelf. Jones pulled it out and knew by the shape and heft of its contents what was inside. He reached in and pulled out a .45 automatic pistol. He pulled back the slide and a live round popped out of the chamber. Danny caught it in the air.

"The lockers alongside, which of them belong to new people?"

Danny looked at Bucky's list. "Not fifteen. That's Donesec's. Seventeen belongs to Ray Collins. He signed up four weeks ago."

"Seventeen has a padlock on it too, another new Wahler. Let's see what's in it."

Seventeen's padlock opened more easily. Inside, they found similar clothing, and another automatic. "What do you think, Jonesey?"

"I think there's a plan in the works. I can't see all around it yet, but these two goons are a part of it."

"So, we tell Skitch, then what?"

"We tell Skitch what we found, but we don't move on these two yet. Let it play out a while, so we can watch them, but in the meantime, let's pull the dogs' teeth." Jones tripped the automatic's release and the clip dropped from the handle of Mateosky's pistol. He thumbed out the bullets one by one and shoved the clip back into the .45. Danny did the same for Collins's gun, and they put the pistols back where they found them.

"Let's see what's in the other lockers."

Most of the lockers had little of interest, except for one that had over five hundred dollars in bills no bigger than a five, one with three sets of loaded dice, and one with a substantial collection of Mexican postcards showing prostitutes plying their trade with tattooed men and occasionally, women.

"This locker's not assigned, but it has a padlock on it," Danny said, pointing to locker nineteen.

Jones opened the padlock and found the locker empty except for a small tin box at the back of the shelf. He recognized the logo of the British sailor framed by ropes: Player's Navy Cut Cigarettes. He held it slantwise to the light and saw no smudges on the shiny surface. It had been wiped clean. He opened the lid and found it was filled with waxed paper bindles of white powder. He tore one open, wet his forefinger and took a sample from the envelope. He touched it to his tongue. "Heroin. High-grade."

"Holy shit."

Jones dropped the open bindle into his pocket and closed the tin. "Can you get Skitch on the phone? We need to talk."

XV

"Heroin?" Skitch slammed his fist onto his desk. "Jesus Christ, we don't allow that stuff here. This is our town; you don't shit where you sleep."

"What about Mary Jane, or coke?" Jones said, "Does the operation deal any drugs at all?"

"We've kept it out of here. Sure, some people might bring in their own supply from the city or other places, or grow their own reefer out in the woods, but we don't sell it, and we don't tolerate it."

"We've sent more than one son of a bitch for a swim for trying to get it started here." Dodie plucked a bindle from the tin. "Mostly small-timers, hop-heads trying to hook other people to feed their own habits. I'm no expert on the subject. What do you figure this batch is worth?"

"I don't know about Pennsylvania, but in L.A., you're looking at a couple of grand on the street." Jones pointed to the sealed bindle in Dodie's hand. That's not some hop-head's handiwork. It's professional quality and quantity."

"So, somebody's trying to start a drug trade in Brownsville?" Skitch said.

Jones shook his head. "No, somebody's trying to make it look like you're starting a drug trade in Brownsville. One phone call to tip the law, and I don't mean the locals on your payroll, I mean the Feds, and they come in with a warrant, search the lockers, and you're down the chute. All the politicians in the world couldn't save you."

"That'd still be a tall order to get a warrant to search this place."

"Not if it's an active crime scene. Maybe that's where Mateosky and Collins come in."

"You think they're undercover agents?"

"My gut says no." Jones turned to Danny. "What do you know about those two?"

"Nothing, really. They signed up a month or so ago, separate from each

"So, somebody's trying to start a drug trade in Brownsville?"

other. They come in, work out, don't talk to each other or anybody else, for that matter."

"Well, they definitely are a pair," Jones said. "Their guns were identical, and so were the bullets. The serial numbers on the automatics were from the same run. One possibility is they were planning a hit on you, Skitch, or you, Dodie, with guns that were already here. That'd bring the cops running and open the door for them to search the gym and eventually the whole joint. It looks to me that somebody wants to bring down your whole operation. I'm betting it's outsiders."

"I agree, but I can't go to New Ken for help with this on the chance that it's their play. So what do we do?" Skitch asked.

"We watch and wait. If we're lucky they won't check on the heroin; they won't want to call attention to the locker, and they'll find their weapons right where they left them and won't check the ammo. If we're lucky. Danny and I'll hang out at the gym tomorrow, and if nothing pops, we can follow either or both of them and see where they go and who they talk to. In the meantime, what'll you do with the junk?"

"I have an idea of my own," Skitch said. Let's replace it with sugar, or alum, or something that looks good and put the tin back where you found it."

"I like that idea," Jones said, "but I was asking what you plan to do with a couple grand worth of heroin?"

Skitch smiled for the first time that night. "There'll be some happy carp in the Mon River tonight."

XVI

PARIS

The passage between the two houses was carefully concealed beneath an artful application of plaster and three layers of wallpaper. De Lancre worked at it carefully, making no more noise than a mouse gnawing a hole for itself. In minutes, an opening the size and dimensions of a small doorway was outlined in the wall. Simmons ran his knife around the opening and found that that section of the wall, lath and plaster was crafted to be removable. His blade hit metal, a hinge, then another. On the other side of the hidden door, his blade ticked on metal once again, a latch. He prodded at it carefully with the tip of his knife.

Without warning the latch clicked and the hidden door swung wide into No. 324. The men sprang back, drawing their pistols, expecting a hail of bullets, but nothing happened.

"Go, my friend," Simmons told de Lancre. "*Vivez pour combattre un autre jour.*"

Live to fight another day. Hennessey's motto for the Unit never seemed to be better advice. "Get out now, while you can," Simmons told the Frenchman.

De Lancre shook his head. "*Non, mon ami.* I will be here when you return from *le Bouche d'Enfer.*"

Simmons nodded. "*C'est bon.*" and taking the canvas bag with the explosives, stepped through the doorway. Cyclops swung the door shut, and it all but disappeared; its facing perfectly matched the carved oak panels of a long hallway with a dust coated rug.

Simmons felt his tattoos warming, as they always did in the presence of magic. The men stood still for a full minute and heard nothing inside the dark mansion.

"I hope you can get that panel open again," Simmons whispered.

Cyclops shrugged, and put his palms to the wood. He closed his eyes briefly then ran his index finger around a carved rose. He turned the flower, and the latch clicked again. Simmons nodded and signaled Cyclops to follow him.

At the end of the hallway they found a kitchen, long unused, thick dust on the shelves and the enormous cast iron stove. The floor, however, showed the passage of many boots. They crept from room to room on the ground floor and found nothing. The house had been stripped of anything that could be carried away years before, and only the bare walls and floors remained.

Pistols drawn, Simmons and Cyclops climbed the stairs to the second floor. The higher they climbed, the warmer Simmons' tattoos grew. The rooms at the front of the second floor were as empty as those on the first. As they crept toward the rear, Simmons felt the itch at the base of his skull, the Sight. It showed him a blur to his left, a blur with fangs and claws.

It was a wolf, but not a wolf. It stood on two legs and had arms that ended in furred hands with hooked claws. He wheeled and reflexively fired at a snarling shape that leapt at him from a shadowy doorway, but it kept coming. The man-wolf collided with him chest to chest and knocked him on his back. He held its head away from his throat by handfuls of its thick dark fur as its paws raked at his shoulders.

Cyclops put his pistol at the base of the creature's skull and fired two shots into its head. The man-wolf gave a sort of sigh, its eyes rolled back in its head, and it fell off Simmons and lay still. A second man-wolf and a third appeared at the end of the hallway. Before they could charge, the Americans fired, and the beast men fell dead.

Again, silence. "That's why there are no Nazi sentries," Simmons said, prodding one of the dead wolf-men with the toe of his boot. "By one, by two, and by three."

"I thought these things only came out when the moon was full." Cyclops spoke in hushed tones.

"That's true, if they're real. But these are humans, or were; the Nazis turn men into monsters with surgery in a laboratory. I've seen the place."

"Tell me about it sometime."

"Someday when the story's declassified."

They dragged the corpses through a doorway and found themselves in a formal dining room with a gaping hole in its ceiling where the chandelier had been removed. "Nowhere to hide these bodies in case someone comes back," Cyclops hissed.

"Wait," Simmons said, pointing. "There." In the corner, they saw the brass handle of a door that opened onto a dumbwaiter. Cyclops tugged at the rope, and the platform began to rise from the kitchen. They set the brake, piled the dead man-wolves onto it and closed the door.

At the end of the hallway, the passage intersected another one that led through the center of the mansion. Halfway across was a double door. "The ball room," Cyclops whispered, "if our information is correct."

As they approached the doorway, Simmons felt his tattoos begin to gently vibrate. He knew if he could see through his clothing, that they would be glowing a dull red. Pistols at the ready, each took a handle and at Cyclops' nod, the pair pulled the doors wide and stared in amazement at what lay beyond.

The *Sylléktis* towered over them, thirty feet tall; its apex reached through the ceiling and disappeared into the darkened chamber above where a section of the floor had been removed. The intricate assembly of bones was surrounded by steel scaffolding. Masonry tools and an empty mortar trough stood in a corner.

O Sylléktis was a perfect blend of majesty, beauty, and horror. Simmons had seen ossuary chapels in different parts of Europe, where human bones had been fashioned into intricate sculptures: arches, chandeliers, a coat of arms, and even whole walls of *memento mori*, but the size and intricacy of *O Sylléktis* reached far beyond the scope of any he had ever seen.

An arch of femurs decorated with skeletal hands opened to the interior of the cone. Inside, they saw a throne built of interlaced bones and like the throne in the drawing, capped with a line of skulls.

Simmons drew a tiny Minox camera from his pocket and began snapping photos of the structure.

Cyclops stared as if transfixed by the blasphemous assembly. "It's amazing." He stepped forward and reached out his hand to touch one of the bones. Simmons grabbed him by the back of the coat and yanked him away. "Don't touch the damned thing. Who knows what it will do."

Cyclops shook his head like a wet dog. "Yeah, you're right. I just forgot myself for a second."

The pair left the ballroom and climbed the stair to the third floor.

"There's the baize door, just like Cram described it." Cram had portrayed the door as covered in moth-eaten green baize, and as heavy as that of a safe. In the intervening years, the moths had all but stripped the door to its bare slab of blackened oak. To Simmons' surprise, the door was not locked, and swung silently inward on well-oiled hinges.

They found themselves in a cubical anteroom, but unlike Cram's description of figureless black walls, runic symbols, most of which Simmons recognized as ancient Norse figures from Hitler's vaunted Aryan heritage, adorned the black walls and ceiling in stark white strokes. At the far end of the antechamber was another door.

The room beyond was exactly as Cram had described it, a round domed chamber with stars in the ceiling and the enormous figure of a nude red woman, as Cram put it, "kneeling, her legs reaching out along the floor on either side, her head touching the lintel of the door through which we had entered, her arms forming its sides, with the forearms extended and stretching along the walls until they met the long feet."

Instead of the pentagram in the floor, the apex of the *Sylléktis* thrust through a round hole to project nearly to the white egg-like object that dangled from the red woman's navel by a delicate chain. Cyclops stood staring at the apex, awestruck. Simmons shook his shoulder. "Snap out of it, come on."

One more door. Simmons held his breath and pushed it open. As soon as he did, the ammoniac stench of rotting flesh poured out, making his eyes water. He shined his torch around the room. The walls were brass plate, green with verdigris, and in the center of the room, an altar of porphyry stood, capped by a basalt pedestal. Around the room, bodies were stacked waist high like cordwood. Those at the bottom more skeleton than corpse

with only scraps of flesh remaining, and those at the top, though more recently dead, were shriveled like people Simmons had seen who starved to
death in concentration camps, skin stretched taut over their bones.

"These skeletons are complete," Cyclops said. "Why didn't they use their
bones to build the *Sylléktis*?"

"Maybe they served a different purpose. Did you notice; there are no
flies." Simmons shined the beam of his light on one of the corpses. "No
maggots. Even the scavengers shun this place. Let's get out of here."

On the ground floor, they set the explosives on shelves near the kitchen
ceiling where they calculated the blast would go off directly under the
Sylléktis. As he was wiring the last of the detonators, Simmons said, "I'll
set the timer for fifteen minutes. That should get us back into the sewers
before it blows." He turned his head, and he saw that Cyclops was gone. In
his gut, Simmons knew where he'd find him.

Before he even reached the second floor, Simmons could feel the vibra-
tion in his skin, and a low humming sound came from the back of the
mansion. He rounded the corner of the upstairs hallway and saw that the
ballroom doors were open, and a dull violet glow shone from within. He
looked through the doorway and saw Cyclops sitting on the throne in the
center of the *Sylléktis*.

Simmons started into the room and fell back, excruciating pain lancing
his arms and torso. His tattoos felt on fire. On the throne, Cyclops' eyes
opened wide, and he began to moan. Patches of smoke drifted from his
sleeves then one of his tattoos burst into flame through his German uniform. The *Sylléktis* began to quiver, and the purple glow became brighter.
At the same time, Cyclops' body began to shrivel, like a fly being sucked
dry by a spider. The sculpture was draining his body and his soul.

Simmons looked upward through the ceiling and saw a pair of blazing
eyes staring down at him from the peak of the sculpture. Cyclops' long
moan became a ragged scream as flames burst from his collar. Simmons
raised his pistol and fired a bullet through his partner's head.

Silence fell. The *Sylléktis* began to shake as if with rage, and the purple
faded into darkness. The flare of Simmons' tattoos flickered out like a candle. The floor shook under his feet. He turned and ran down the stairs and
back into the kitchen where he reset the timer to detonate in five minutes
instead of fifteen and started the clock. As he ran for the hallway, he heard
shouting from the vestibule and the pounding of boots on the parquet
floors.

Simmons found the hidden door and turned the rose. The latch clicked, and the heavy wooden panel swung into the hallway just in time to stop a burst of gunfire from a German soldier. Simmons dove through the opening and pulled the door shut on an arm with a pistol that fired blindly into the portal. The third shot hit Simmons' calf, and he grunted in pain but didn't dare let go of the door.

De Lancre shoved into the opening beside him and pressed the barrel of his pistol against the gunman's wrist. He fired two, three, four shots at point blank range until the hand with the pistol fell from a spurting, gory stump. The arm withdrew, Simmons felt the door lock, and de Lancre dragged him down the cellar stairs.

The front door to No. 326 splintered above, and Simmons heard the pounding of feet on the floor overhead.

"Hurry!" De Lancre held the trap door to the subcellar open. Simmons began clambering down the ladder but his leg gave out and he fell heavily to the floor below. De Lancre scrambled through the opening and closed the lid behind him. Simmons was getting weak from the loss of blood, and de Lancre had to shove him through the hole into the sewer.

He lay on the stone walkway. As de Lancre took his hand to pull him to his feet, the explosion rocked the tunnel. A cloud of dust shot from the hole in the tunnel wall, and the boom echoed through the myriad passages of the sewer. That and something that followed, a roar, a bellow of rage that filled Simmons' ears and his head for a second, then faded like the explosion.

De Lancre put his shoulder under Simmons' armpit. He half dragged, half carried him down the stone path away from No. 324.

"What of Cyclops?"

Simmons shook his head. "Gone. I couldn't save him."

De Lancre turned his head to look him in the eye and said, "But you— *Vivez pour combattre un autre jour.*"

XVII

PENNSYLVANIA

The Ford's engine roared as Jones made the climb up the Summit, part of the Blue Ridge Mountains.

U.S. 40 wound a curving path up the steep slope to the top and into the forests of the Chestnut Ridge where Jones had an appointment with Coakee to see to his car. Like an Old West Cowboy took good care of his horse, Jones took good care of his coupe.

The mountains looked like a rumpled patchwork quilt with its swaths of Autumn orange, yellow and red interspersed with the dark green of pines, a look a painter would be hard put to capture with a brush and oils. Mist rose from some of the dales, giving the scene an otherworldly look. He remembered a quote from a book he'd read by Dickens, *Nicholas Nickleby*: "Nature gives to every time and season some beauties of its own." Some things are too large for men to ruin, he thought, that or men are simply too busy ruining each other.

The morning air was crisp blowing through windows Jones kept rolled part way down to hide the bullet holes. Coakee would take care of the glass and the holes in the fenders, but what Jones wanted more was to have the master mechanic fine tune the engine. The Ford had served him well, and he wanted to keep it that way.

Jones turned the radio dial as he drove; searching for a station that played the kind of music he'd learned to appreciate in L.A. but had no luck. Local stations faded in and out from ridge to ridge, and the strongest signal he could find was KDKA out of Pittsburgh; they didn't play hot jazz or blues, so Jones had to settle for big band.

At the top of the mountain, he passed the great white Summit Hotel, looking as if an oversized Louisiana plantation house had dropped from the sky and landed on the ridge. He'd spent a night there once in love with a woman who betrayed him and died the next day. As the hotel faded in his rear view mirror, so did the memory.

On the other side of the ridge, Jones took a road to his right that plunged into dense forest. The buttery sunlight dimmed as the Ford rolled beneath a canopy of trees whose limbs reached across the road to touch each other. He took one turn after another, each leading to a road worse than the one before. Coakee had his own lane leading to the highway that was as smooth as poured concrete, but it was closed off with padlocked gates to keep out trespassers. Jones could have picked the locks easily, but thought better of it.

Finally, at the end of a mile or more of ruts and rocks that threatened to rip the oil pan from the engine, Jones came to a stretch of road groomed like a clay tennis court. At its end, he found a barn sided with rough planks grayed by the weather and surrounded by a tangle of brush, brambles and sumac trees almost as tall as the barn itself.

He rolled onto the packed bare earth in front of the barn, and four loud, huge dogs came boiling out of the doorless hulk of a rusting delivery van beside the barn. They circled his car, snarling and barking, and Jones knew better than to open the door. One of the mutts, a dog that looked like a cross between a mastiff and an alligator, went on its hind legs and stuck its barking head through the open window. Jones was rolling it up when a sharp whistle made the dogs stop barking and sit on their haunches awaiting further orders.

It had been two years since Jones had seen Earl Coakee, and as hard as it was to believe, the man was bigger than the last time they'd met. Coakee was a good six-foot-six and weighed over three hundred pounds. His ham-sized hands bulged from the cuffs of a grease stained coverall, and his torso rested like a haystack on a pair of tree trunks. His stringy red hair flowed from beneath a red leather ball cap and blended seamlessly into an equally stringy beard.

"C.O. Jones," the red faced giant said with a chuckle. "Long time no see." He crouched and petted the dogs, scratching their ears and bellies then clapped his hands and said, "Kennel." The dogs trotted back to the van without another sound.

Jones opened the door and stepped out of the car. "Your dogs don't like me any more than they ever did, Coakee."

"Hell, they don't like anybody. They'd go after me if I didn't feed them regular. They're too damned lazy to hunt up their own food."

"Sounds like a match made in heaven."

The tip of Coakee's little finger didn't quite fit in the bullet holes in the front fender. "I see you're still breathing, so I suppose the shooter isn't." He squatted beside the car and peered into the wheel well. "You're lucky the bullets didn't blow the tire or hit anything important. Cars're like people; hit a fuel line's like hittin' an artery."

He stood up, more gracefully than one might expect for somebody his size and bulk. "How's she running, Jones?"

"Pretty good. I drove wide open all the way from California, and never a complaint from the engine."

Coakee grinned with pride. "Try that with one off the showroom floor. Pull her in."

He rolled the door away and Jones drove the Ford into the barn. The ramshackle exterior hid the most complete and pristine machine shop Jones had ever seen. The concrete floor was swept clean, and every tool hung in its assigned place on the wall. Three cars in various states of repair stood to the left, like patients in a hospital ward. Jones saw a pair of legs sticking out below the running board of a Buick sedan and another mechanic leaning under the hood of a Cadillac that looked like a crocodile ready to bite him in half.

Coakee walked around the Ford. "Window glass should be easy to come by. I might find it at the junkyard, but if I don't, I'll get it cut downtown. I'll get Jack to take care of the holes and this crease in the roof. She'll look like new in a day or two."

Jones peeled two hundred dollar bills from his roll. "Take this up front. We can settle up later if that doesn't cover it. While you have it, go over the whole car and fix anything it needs."

Coakee laughed. "You buy a car I built, Jones, it's like marrying my daughter if I had one. I know you respect a good machine; I'll see she runs right."

Jones walked out with Coakee, and he saw the dogs sitting on their haunches outside the barn. Their heads turned as one like a school of fish turning in the water as Coakee led him to a green Mercury roadster with a tan convertible top. Coakee handed him the keys. "This'll do you for a day or two." Jones scribbled the phone number of the pool room on a leaf of his notebook and tore it out. "You can reach me here or leave a message when the car's ready."

"Always a pleasure doing business with you, Jones."

Jones thought about putting the top down on the roadster to enjoy one of the last days of Autumn sun, but caution overruled the whim. In his business, the less exposed he was, the better.

XVII

Jones enjoyed driving, especially by himself; it gave him time to think. The incidents in and around Brownsville seemed unrelated, almost random, but their timing made them less likely to be coincidence. If someone wanted to take over an entrenched operation, it made sense that the first step was to put it on shaky ground. People who paid for protection expected it. Complacent law enforcement couldn't look aside when the Feds rolled in. And an organization whose respect was founded on fear and intimidation couldn't maintain it for long if the perception of control eroded.

Then there was the heroin. If the local mob didn't traffic in it, someone else might see a ripe opportunity in Brownsville. Jones had only experienced heroin once, and that was during his training for the OSS when Hennessey insisted that they be exposed to every drug available so that they would know how to handle them if they encountered one or another of them in the field. He understood that the euphoria heroin induced, even in a mild dose, could be an irresistible lure to a weaker mind or a troubled soul.

Skitch's prohibition of the drug in the spirit of protecting the community was noble, but Jones understood that what spawned in the cities would, sooner or later, take root in the smallest towns in the country. You can't live other people's lives for them, he thought, and you sure as hell can't protect people from themselves.

Danny would be keeping an eye on the gym, watching to see if Mateosky and Collins came, singly or together, and whether either of them went into the lockers. In the meantime, Jones wanted to talk with Tony Rocco.

At twenty to noon Jones parked the roadster right behind Rocco's cream colored Nash. On the second floor of the building, the apartment was easy to find. It was the one with the new door jamb, replacing the one the cops kicked in after the bank job.

When he gave Jones the address, Dodie told him that the bag man never woke up before lunch time, and, as advertised, Jones's knock got him out of bed. He came to the door in striped pajamas and a red velour bathrobe. His slicked back hair stuck out at odd angles in patches like so many cowlicks.

"Jones?" Rocco blinked, still half asleep and a little hung over. "What the hell are you doing in Brownsville?"

"Back on the payroll, Tony."

Rocco yawned and his mouth gaped open like the MGM lion without the roar. He slipped off the safety chain and opened the door. "C'mon in."

"Nice digs."

He gave Jones a half side smile. "Yeah, Marcene has good taste."

The furniture in the apartment was a lot more expensive than Jones would have expected from anyone in Brownsville except a crook. Marcene had good taste, all right. Jones imagined the two of them strolling through a furniture store in the middle of the afternoon, picking out a leather sofa, overstuffed easy chairs, lamps, end tables, and an Oriental rug then a truck in the alley backing up to the store's loading dock at two a.m.

"So what's up, Jones?" Like many western Pennsylvanians, Tony swallowed the letter H, turning words like "them" into "tem" and "fifth" into "fift."

"I need you to tell me about this robbery frame."

"I don't know too much you probably don't already know. The sonofa-bitch dressed up to look like me. In the confusion and the smoke, nobody really got a good look at his face. The kicker was him driving off in my car. I ain't stupid enough to use a car everybody in town knows is mine for a getaway. Then park it outside my front door and go to sleep? And it wasn't even a big score."

"How much?"

"I heard it was about six hundred bucks, although the papers quoted the bank president as saying it was over a grand. I figure the difference went in his pocket. I tell you what, though, I almost wish I was there to see those guards trying to get through the revolving door. I hear the bank's replac-ing it with some kind of heavy security doors."

"How about your car? Where was it parked that morning?"

"Right where you saw it today. That's my space," Rocco said with pride. "Nobody parks in it but me."

"No one saw somebody messing with your car or driving it away?"

Rocco shook his head. "Nah. You know the score around here, Jones. Nobody sees nothin'."

"But somebody stole your Nash. Was the door lock jimmied?"

"No, but I almost never lock it up around here anyway. Everybody knows it's my car. Nobody in his right mind would mess with it."

Jones saw that the bag man's arrogance was born of complacency. Nothing had changed for so long that people expected that things would always be the same. "So, he hot-wired it?"

"No, that's the weird thing. None of the wires were pulled, no tool marks, no damage."

"So he used the key. Did you leave it in the ignition, or under the visor, or anywhere else the guy could find it?"

Rocco gave Jones the lopsided grin again. "Even I ain't that confident, Jones."

"Tony?" A woman's voice from the bedroom. Jones looked up to see Marcene framed in the doorway in a pink see through negligee. Her eyes were puffy from sleep and her short blonde hair looked like a bird's nest. The rest of her in the filmy nightie looked pretty good, though. Tony had good taste too.

Tony turned around and saw the show. "Go put some clothes on and make us a pot of coffee, willya."

"Make it yourself." Marcene pouted and retreated into the bedroom, slamming the door. Tony started out of his chair as if he were going to punish her behavior, but sat back down, either too tired or too hung over to deal with her at the moment.

"Okay, spare keys. Do you keep any here in the apartment?"

"I had one spare I got from the dealer when I bought the car, but Marcene lost it. I had another one made. It's over there in the desk drawer." He pointed to a walnut secretary across the room.

"Was that key missing?"

"It was there when I looked for it, but that was after Skitch bailed me out. I guess somebody could have broken in here and swiped it, but when would they have put it back? The cops were in here the whole time tearing the place apart looking for the loot. Marcene was here too, giving them hell."

"Maybe they put it back before the robbery. You know you're lucky."

"Lucky? How?"

"The robber could have thrown the loot in the rumble seat, even part of it in the bank wrappers, if this was just a play to frame you. He wanted the money and not the blame. While the cops were rousting you, he got away. Let me have that spare key for a day or two. How many locksmiths are there in town?"

"Two of them, Matthews and Shrenk. Shrenk made the key."

"I'll pay them both a visit."

XVIII

PARIS

Simmons lay for two days in the Unit's safe house. The gunshot wound in his leg had developed sepsis from the sewer water, and he quickly became fevered and delirious. He tossed in the sweat soaked sheets drifting in and out of consciousness. In his dreams, he saw the glowing *Sylléktis*, Cyclops' shriveling body, and the blazing eyes peering at him from above.

On the third day, his eyelids fluttered open to the sight of a tattered blind at a window beside the bed, swaying in and out on a mild breeze. He turned his eyes away from the casement and saw de Lancre sitting in a chair beside the bed.

"Welcome back to the world, *mon ami.*"

Simmons tried to raise himself on his elbow but was too weak. "How long have I been out?"

"Two days, more or less."

"Where am I?"

"Paris, in a secure place."

Simmons struggled to focus his eyes. When he tried to fix them on an object, the room seemed to slide sideways. He gave up and shut them again. "And the mission?"

"Successful. No. 324 *Rue des Pauvres* is gone. The explosion collapsed the house into itself, and all that remains is a mound of rubble."

"And *O Sylléktis*?"

De Lancre chuckled. "Bones rained down on the city for three blocks in every direction. The whole neighborhood looked like a charnel house."

"I owe you my life."

"Paris owes you as well. At this stage, we no longer tally debt."

Simmons was silent for a while then said. "There is one debt still to be paid."

In another day he could get out of bed. Two days after that he began to recover his strength. The care the sympathetic doctor the Resistance provided couldn't give Simmons the treatment he might have gotten in a hospital, so his healing was slow, but without it, he surely would have died.

Stengler had left the city, and likely left the planet. The SS had little tolerance for failure. But the Nazis couldn't replace Chirac. He remained somewhere near Paris, under protective guard now that the SS understood that the Unit was onto their plans.

"There is troubling news as well," de Lancre said. The Nazis have crews of conscripted men removing the debris. They are working at it like ants night and day."

O Sylléktis had been destroyed, but under the rubble, the nexus of power remained, the crossing of force lines that had been there before time and would be there after it ended. The Nazis were going to replace No. 324 with a new building and reconstruct the monstrosity that sucked the life and soul from men to drive its evil.

Hennessey is wrong, Simmons thought. Some brands of magic are evil by their nature, more than the use to which men put them. *O Sylléktis* is one. Chirac must be eliminated before he can build another.

XIX

BROWNSVILLE

Fiddle's Confectionary was a diner that sat under the bridge connecting Fayette and Washington counties, Brownsville and West Brownsville, where Maria Bronski and her husband had their grocery store. Jones had second thoughts about walking into the place but went anyway. The food was good and it was cheap.

The place hadn't changed in two years; checkerboard tile on the floor, pedestal stools along the counter, milk glass globes hanging by chains from the ceiling and a bulb was still burnt out in one of them. The warm aroma of fry cooking wafted from the kitchen. He picked up a copy of the *Telegraph* someone had left on the counter and slid into a booth.

"What'll you have, Mac?"

The waitress was a short woman in a white uniform, her red hair pulled back in a snood. "Mabel" was stitched on her breast pocket in red. Her teeth were crooked, but her smile was genuine

"Do you still have the roast beef sandwich with mashed potatoes and gravy?"

She nodded, scribbling on her pad. "Uh-huh. Anything else?"

"Yeah, a side order of corn and coffee."

As she walked away, Jones felt a pang of sadness over another woman who'd waited on him in Fiddle's two years before. He'd opened his heart to Ellie, and she played him for the bad guys. She threw herself between Jones and Jan Hutz, her boss and lover, thinking Jones wouldn't shoot. Ellie was wrong.

She deserved to die for her duplicity and her part in a plot that would have set unbridled evil loose on an unsuspecting world. Jones reminded himself of that fact and picked up the newspaper.

Nothing much in the news. The six week Australian coal miners' strike that took over a half million workers off the job was over, but CIO Steelworker strikes took over 90,000 workers off the job, and the strikes were spreading. A Congressional report said that the Marshall Plan's economic success was "in jeopardy," and blamed the "peculiar postwar state of mind of the average Frenchman." From what Jones knew of the Frenchmen he'd fought alongside in the war, they were a proud people, and he understood that they resented the paternalistic handouts and the

Jones picked up the newspaper. Nothing much in the news.

implied demands that accompanied them from an upstart country not even two hundred years old.

Mabel looked over his shoulder as she poured his coffee. "You know, that Marshall guy was born right down the road in Uniontown. Cream and sugar?"

"No, thanks. I'll take it black."

He turned to the sports page. The main story was about Ezzard Charles, as it had been for the past week. In two more days, he'd meet challenger Pat Valentino at the Cow Palace in California to defend his title. He'd won it fighting Jersey Joe Walcott in June at Wrigley Field, but Boxing was like playing King of the Hill. As soon as you hit the top, somebody's ready to try to knock you back down again.

Mabel set his plate down and Jones set down the newspaper. The food was as good as ever, even if the memories weren't.

XX

The pool room was busy in the early afternoon. Jones saw Skitch and Dodie playing at their personal table in the back corner. Skitch, in vest and shirtsleeves, was bent over the table lining up a shot. He squinted through the smoke of a cigarette hooked in the corner of his mouth. Jones waited out of courtesy, not wanting to distract him.

Skitch slid the stick between his fingers, once, twice, and on the third time, gently nudged the cue ball. It rolled slowly through a seemingly impossible space between the purple four ball and the rail, barely caromed off the bumper, and went on to nudge the eight ball into a corner pocket.

Dodie swore under his breath and reached under the table for the rack. His shirt today was the shade of orange Jones associated with the last embers of a burned out log.

"Jones," said Skitch. "Wanna play a game of cut throat with us?"

Jones shook his head. "No thanks. I'd be the one gets his throat cut. I'm heading up to the gym."

"News?"

"Not a lot to talk about yet. I do need to ask, though. Is there anything I should know about the locksmiths in town?"

"We have both of them on the pad, Matthews and Shrenk; spread the business around, keep them both happy. Keep their mouths shut."

"Good to know."

"What's up, Jones?"

"Maybe nothing, but I have to check it out."

Skitch nodded and turned to Dodie. "Your break." Then to Jones, "Stop up later."

Jones left as Dodie broke with a crack like a gunshot and a curse.

Upstairs, the gym was as busy as the pool room. With the mills and the mines running rotating shifts, the gym could have been open around the clock if Skitch wanted to run it that way. Instead, the men came when they could, some still grimy from their shifts at the mines or the coke ovens. So many men dreaming they might get a shot at glory in the ring; maybe escape the hard labor that wore their fathers to the nub like a great grinding wheel by taking all the punishment at once instead.

Danny was working a heavy bag, stripped to the waist, his torso slick with sweat. He ended with a series of combinations and caught the swinging bag between his gloves. "Hey, Jonesey." He caught the lace of one glove between his teeth and undid the bow. He put the glove in his armpit and pulled his hand free. "The bag's good, but it only goes so far. You know judo?"

Jones gave Danny a thin smile. "A little."

"They taught us a lot of hand to hand technique in the Corps, but I've gotten rusty since V-J Day. Maybe you and I could go a few rounds some time."

"I'm not sure I want everybody in the place to see everything I can do."

Danny undid his other glove. "You may be right about that."

"Did Mateosky or Collins come in here today?"

He shook his head. "Nope. I asked around, and Collins works at Hillman welding barges. Mateosky's a coal miner swinging shifts at Thompson 3. I'll be around to see whether either of them comes in."

"I'm going to work out myself. Talk with you later."

Jones changed into his cotton sweats and canvas gym shoes. He started by skipping rope for ten minutes as a warm up then moved to the dumbbells. He worked high repetitions at low weight for tone and endurance then went to the bench to work with a heavy barbell. He did three sets of bench presses with two hundred pounds. He could have pushed a lot more, but as he told Danny, better to not show it off.

By the time he was done, Jones's shirt was soaked across his chest from armpit to armpit. He was ready to hit the showers when a big man in work clothes came in. he was at least six-foot-five and built like a fire plug. His face, under a shock of graying hair, was a ruddy shade with a fleshy nose over a pair of thick lips.

"Who wants to fight?" the man said.

Jones walked over to the corner where Danny was leaning, smoking a cigarette. "Who's that guy?"

"That's Chester. He comes in every week or so and gets in the ring with anybody who'll fight him."

"Is he a drunk, a punchy old pug?"

"Nah. He just likes to fight. He works at the roundhouse. He started coming around maybe a year ago, and nobody minds him. He can't fight for shit, but the young guys get in the ring with him for practice. They beat him bloody and he goes away 'til next time he gets the itch."

One of the boxers stepped away from the speed bag where he was being watched by an older man in a rumpled suit. "I'll take you on, Chester." The challenger was a swarthy man with a full head of black hair and tendons that stood out like ropes under his skin.

"Who's he?" Jones said.

"Art Rizzoli. He's won a few bouts, thinks he's hot stuff. The old guy's his manager, Tommy Biancardi. Nobody wants to spar with Art. He likes to hurt people."

Across the floor, Jones saw Rizzoli arguing with his manager. He turned to walk away and Biancardi grabbed his shoulder. Rizzoli shook the hand off and headed for the ring. "Come on, Chester, get your gloves on." Art grabbed the ropes and pulled himself into the ring. Chester held out his hands and one of the pugs laced a pair of sparring gloves on him.

"Rizzoli's still wearing the weighted bag gloves," Jones said. "He'll murder the old man."

"Hey, Rizzoli, put on the right gloves," Danny shouted.

"Mind your own business, Hayes, or you'll be next."

Danny started for the ring, but Jones held him back. "Let it go."

"Somebody ring the bell," Rizzoli said.

At ringside, Biancardi held up a dark rubber horseshoe. "Art, at least put in your mouthpiece."

"I won't need it with this tomato can," Rizzoli sneered.

The bell rang. Rizzoli danced from his corner and Chester lumbered bear-like from his. Chester's fists were like hams, but he carried them too low and too wide to protect himself. He waded in, swinging one fist then the other at Rizzoli's head. The boxer dodged the blows easily, and landed a vicious combination to Chester's face, opening a cut under his right eye.

Chester swung again, this time catching Rizzoli's shoulder and knocking him off balance. He staggered back and found his footing. The crowd that had gathered around the ring hooted in derision. Rizzoli's expression changed from arrogance to anger. He drove into Chester delivering combinations to the older man's chest and stomach. Chester put his gloves over his bloody face but didn't have the savvy to tuck his elbows together to protect his torso.

Rizzoli pounded at Chester until he dropped his arms and the boxer delivered a punch that put Chester's teeth through his lower lip. Chester put his gloves over his face and sagged against the ropes. Rizzoli turned toward his deriders, a smug grin on his face.

Chester came off the ropes and swung a roundhouse that caught Rizzoli on the side of his jaw. The sound was like an axe splitting a stump. Rizzoli fell hard, and from the crazy angle of his jaw, Jones could see that it was broken.

Biancardi leaped into the ring and bent over his fighter. He stood and pointed at his finger at Chester. "You crazy Bo-hunk, what the hell do think you're doing? The fight was over."

Chester licked at his bloody lip. "Nobody rang the bell."

Biancardi's eyes blazed. "I'll ring the bell for your goddamned funeral." Biancardi pulled a knife from his sleeve and started for Chester. Jones grabbed a five pound kettle bell from the floor and threw it like a baseball through the ropes and into the ring. It caught Biancardi in the shoulder, and he dropped the knife. Before he could pick it up again, a half dozen people had swarmed through the ropes and slammed him to the canvas.

"That was quick thinking, Jonesey. I'll go get Skitch," Danny said and disappeared down the stairs into the pool room.

Amid all the noise and confusion, Chester climbed out of the ring, put on his denim work coat, and walked down the stairs and out the door. From the window, Jones saw him cross the street, get into a rusty Chevrolet sedan and drive away.

XXI

PARIS

Eight days after *O Sylléktis* was destroyed, Simmons was walking well enough to consider going after Chirac. He had thought of little else during his convalescence in the third floor of the town house the Unit maintained in Paris, and now that he was on his feet again, he wanted nothing more than to kill Chirac and end the mission.

Simmons' updated orders were to kill Chirac and if possible, find and eliminate the magician responsible for controlling *O Sylléktis*. Waiting was the most difficult for Jones, but he'd learned long ago that the worst mistake an operative could make was haste. Hennessey put it simply: Don't hurry; don't worry.

On the tenth day, de Lancre arrived with news. Chirac was sequestered in the *Ville Duchamps*, the manor house of a country estate on a small island in the Seine a few miles north of Paris. The house had been appropriated as a recreational retreat for Nazi officers. "The heavy guard on the island will make our task difficult, but we do have an agent inside. She is one of the prostitutes brought in from time to time to entertain the *Boche* officers."

"Can she get us into the house?"

"That remains to be seen, but in the meantime, she has provided us with the layout of the place. From that, we may be able to form a plan."

"Chirac is definitely there?"

"As of yesterday, yes. Collette saw him then, and once two days before. She would have given her life to kill him then, but she never got close enough. The prostitutes are not for him."

"I need eyes on the place. I'd call for an air strike, but the odds are that the bombers would never make it past the Atlantic Wall and the Luftwaffe." The German anti-aircraft bunkers that lined the French coast were an effective impediment to Allied aircraft, and the Nazi fighter pilots were legendary in their skills. "And with my luck, Chirac would be gone the day before the strike. I have to see him die to know that this is finally over."

"Then we will mount a reconnaissance mission. The more we know, the more likely we will succeed. In the meantime, Collette will tell us what she sees. And for now, I have brought you these." de Lancre set a pair of tattered magazines on the table, one the French movie rag *Mon Film*, and the other a copy of *Life Magazine* with a full-cover black and white photo of Fred Astaire dancing with Ginger Rogers.

"In *Mon Film*, you will find photographs of a French Starlet, Marie Mimet taken on the grounds of the *Ville Duchamps* when she was the mistress of the younger Duchamps, the playboy. Most of the pictures were shot by the fountain and in the gardens, but they do show views of the exterior and are useful for scale. The *Life Magazine* contains an article on the Duchamps industrial dynasty and it features two pages of photographs, inside and outside the mansion. Study them well, my friend."

After de Lancre left, Simmons sat until the daylight faded from the window staring at the photographs of *Ville Duchamps*, and then by lamplight until he burned every available detail of the architecture into his brain. If he found Chirac there, Simmons was determined that the collaborator would never leave the island alive.

Two days later, Simmons and de Lancre lay in the brush on the shore of the Seine watching the house and grounds of the *Ville Duchamps*. Simmons took his eyes away from the powerful monocular scope trained on the terrace outside the mansion and rubbed his eye with his knuckles. A pair of uniformed German soldiers, one carrying an MP 40 and the other holding two mastiffs on chains crossed the terrace and disappeared into the shrubbery of the garden.

Simmons had clocked their routine patrol and found that their appearance was random rather than rigidly scheduled. They could reappear in thirty minutes of forty-five, move clockwise around the grounds or the reverse. Tripod machine guns guarded the river at intervals all around the island. Trying to enter the grounds would be a risky proposition at best.

"Do you think Chirac is guarded with magic?"

"Not likely," Simmons said. "Dogs are highly sensitive to its presence, and I've seen all kinds of birds and even a cat on the grounds." Their security is one hundred percent earthly.

"Let me take a turn," de Lancre said. "Rest your eyes."

Simmons rolled away from the scope and de Lancre took his place, but the American's gaze was still fixed on the house in the middle of the river. Their surveillance thus far had been in daylight, and limited to the grounds and the outside of the Gothic mansion three hundred yards away. The sun had set, and soon night would fall and lighted rooms would give them a glimpse of its interior through the lancet windows.

"Look," de Lancre said, "the boat." He turned the monocular on its tripod. A motor launch puttered across the water from the shore to the island, a uniformed soldier at the helm. A pair of SS officers in their leather trench coats sat in the bow.

Simmons timed the crossing with the sweep hand of his wristwatch. One minute forty-two seconds from the shore to the dock at the southern corner of the island. "That may be our best chance," he said. "I can get a clear shot from here at anyone in the boat."

"True, but how long must we wait for Chirac to make the crossing? And how long can we wait?"

"Not much longer. The device may not be a work of art this time, but it would work."

Once Chirac was taken from *Ville Duchamps*, he would not return. He would labor around the clock to rebuild the hideous sculpture before 30 April arrived and with it, the opening of the gate between worlds. If Chirac was to die, it would have to be on the island or on the launch before he reached the shore.

De Lancre returned the scope to the terrace. "Wormwood," he hissed. "Chirac. It is he."

Simmons put his eye to the lens and saw the sculptor standing at the edge of the terrace lighting a briar pipe. A Nazi *oberst* stood beside him, partially blocking him from view. Chirac was wearing a red sweater and khaki trousers, both hanging loosely from his frame, as if they were a child's hand-me-downs from an older brother. Not his own clothes, Simmons guessed. The SS had hustled him out of Paris with no time to pack. The red sweater would make him easy to spot among the grey tunics of the German officers.

As quickly as he appeared, Chirac was gone. He and his companion strolled to the end of the terrace and around the corner of the mansion. "He is here," Simmons said, "Now we just have to figure out how to kill him. For the moment, I'll just watch for a clear shot when we see him again."

Simmons drew a long rifle from his canvas bag. His weapon was a captured Japanese Type 37, the deadly Arisaka sniper rifle with its thirty-one inch barrel, five round magazine and monopod rest. An offset scope was fitted to the left of the barrel for a right-handed shooter. He checked the magazine, worked the bolt, and waited.

Lights came on behind the windows of the mansion. Smoke from the chimneys at the rear of the house told the watchers that the kitchen staff was preparing supper for the guests. Simmons and de Lancre watched for hours as people passed one window or another, but neither caught another glimpse of the baggy red sweater.

The glow from an upstairs room drew Simmons's attention. He trained the scope on an oriel at the north corner of the mansion. Through its diamond window panes, he saw two German officers, stripped to the waist, pouring wine over a nude red-haired woman and licking it from her breasts. A second woman, a buxom blonde joined in the fun, and Simmons turned the scope back to the lower windows, wondering if one of the women was Collette.

Behind the terrace, lay the library. In one of the *Life* photographs, the room was well detailed, lined with bookshelves from floor to ceiling, comfortable chairs, a large, round table, and Tiffany lamps. Here, the windows reached to the ceiling for maximum light, and they afforded Simmons a good view of the interior. The lens was powerful enough that he could see the spines of individual books but not read their titles.

A door opened and Chirac entered alone, still in his red sweater. He crossed the room, passing window to window, and selected an oversized book from one of the shelves. He brought it to the round table and sat facing the window as he opened it. The artist began sketching something Simmons could not see with a pad and pencil.

Chirac looked up and a man in the black uniform of the SS entered. He sat beside Chirac and the two began a conversation.

"This is it," Simmons said. "We may never have a better chance." He opened a canvas case, drew a second rifle from the carry bag, and handed it to the Frenchman. The piece was heavy, bulky, with a hexagonal barrel three feet long and a scope the length of de Lancre's arm. "That's a .45 caliber. Can you hit the center window of the library from here? I can't risk the glass deflecting my shot."

"I think so," de Lancre said. He nodded once. "I must."

Simmons was counting on the instant of surprise when the window shattered, before the startled Chirac would move, to make the kill shot through the empty casement. "Sight it in. Aim for the center. Anywhere you hit it with that round should blow out the whole window and I'll have a clear shot."

"As you say." de Lancre laid the stock across the trunk of a fallen tree and put his eye to the scope.

Simmons laid his cheek against the stock of the Arisaka and peered through the eyepiece. He put the crosshairs at the center of the red sweater and closed his eyes. He took a deep breath through his nose and let it out of his mouth. "Ready?"

"*Oui.*"

"On three." Simmons took another breath. "One, two. Wait."

The center window was blocked by a figure, a man standing with his back to the glass, clasping his hands behind him. His grey tunic identified him as a German officer. Damn it, thought Simmons. "Move, you son of a bitch," he hissed under his breath. "Stay ready, Jacques. As soon as he moves, we'll fire."

After what seemed an eternity, the officer stepped away from the window, and their luck held. The red sweater had not moved from the chair. "One, two, three."

De Lancre's rifle cracked and the report echoed up and down the banks of the river. In one second, the glass of the library exploded, and in the same instant, Simmons's bullet flew through the opening. The shot hit Chirac full in the chest and threw him back in the chair. Simmons worked the bolt of the 37 and fired again, hitting Chirac a second time, and he slumped from the chair under the table. The SS officer leaped to his feet, and before he moved out of view, Simmons put a slug into his gut that spun him halfway around and dropped him to the floor.

The hit was over in four seconds. A minute later across the river, lights came on, and men ran from every direction to the river bank. They all raised weapons, but no one knew where to aim. Commands were shouted and obeyed, but the damage was done, and by the time the Germans realized where the shots had been fired, and machine gun fire raked the brush where Simmons and de Lancre were hiding, they were swimming down the Seine away from *Ville Duchamps* to a waiting boat. In two hours, they were back at the safe house. In a day, Simmons was on his way across the Channel in a Navy submarine pointed to the White Cliffs of Dover.

XXII

BROWNSVILLE

ater Street ran along the river and was protected from all but the most severe flooding by the mile-long shoulder of earth that supported the bed of the Pennsylvania Railroad tracks and doubled as a dike. The trade off for safety was the combined din of bells, horns and the thunder of the big locomotives as they dragged their mile long strings of coal cars through

the town. Still, people lived, worked, and slept as the trains rumbled by.

Jones almost missed Matthews' locksmith shop, tucked between Sam's Shoe Repair and the Sons of Italy social club. He parked the Mercury and crossed the street as a blast from its klaxons announced the approach of yet another northbound freight. A line of rattling hopper cars stretched behind the engine for as far as Jones could see.

A sign in the shop window read: Keys Made Guns Repaired. Good to know, Jones thought as he opened the door.

The shop was narrow and divided in two by a counter. Behind it, shelves rose almost to the ceiling to the left, and set of pigeonholes like hotel mail-boxes stood to the right, leaving an opening to the work area in the back of the shop.

The place was cluttered but clean. The shelves and compartments were packed with locks, hasps, door sets, and related hardware, some new in boxes, others awaiting repair. Through the opening, Jones saw an equally cluttered workbench and a hook board with hundreds of brass key blanks.

"Be right there," a voice called from the back. A woman. Jones saw her from behind, a slim blonde with a ponytail hanging between the shoulders of her grey shop coat as she reached to put something on an overhead shelf. She turned and came to the counter, wiping her hands on a grease-stained rag.

"Can I help you?"

Jones didn't answer right away. He studied the woman's face. Her grey eyes bookended a long straight nose over a perfectly symmetrical mouth, not quite smiling but open just wide enough to show off a perfectly sym-metrical set of front teeth. She wore no makeup, but Jones could see that tricked out for a night on the town, she'd be a beauty.

"I found a key," Jones said. "I was wondering whether you could tell me what it fits."

"Let's see it." She held out her hand. The nails were trimmed to the quick, no polish, and one was split. She held the key in her palm and turned it over, examining the ridges. "It's a car key, a copy, not a manufacturer's original; it's a spare cut from a blank. Could be a couple of makes based on the octagonal bow."

She looked him straight in the eye. "Where'd you find this?"

Nothing shy about this one, Jones thought. "On the sidewalk outside the Odd Fellows Hall," he lied. "If I know what kind of car it belongs to, I can find the owner and give it back to him."

The vestige of a smile faded. "Or you could get in it and drive it away."

"If I wanted to steal a car, I could just walk down the street and try the key 'til I found a fit. Thanks anyway. I guess I'll try elsewhere."

The Sight showed Jones her fingers closing over the key, and he moved so fast she barely saw his hand snatch it away. Her grey eyes glared at him. Jones grinned. "I'll see you next time I need a key made." He nodded toward the sign in the window. "Or a gun repaired." He turned to leave.

"Hey, what's your name, Mister?"

"Jones. C.O. Jones What's yours?"

"Matthews. J. M. Matthews," she said in a mocking imitation.

"Nice to meet you. What's the J. M. stand for?"

"Jenny Marie. What's the C.O. stand for?"

"Co-operative, unlike some people."

Jones looked over his shoulder as he pulled the green convertible away from the curb. He could see Jenny Matthews watching him through the shop window, probably writing down his license number. Some days it was good to drive a borrowed car.

He couldn't imagine her working for Skitch.

Shrenk's shop was up a steep hill from the town Library. It was a stand-alone building, a house whose downstairs was converted to a storefront and the upstairs kept as living quarters. The words on the window pane in gold leaf read: Alvin Shrenk Locksmith and under that: Locks Keys Repairs. No mention of guns. Behind the house, Jones saw a garage. One of the doors was open, revealing a year-old Chevy sedan.

Max Shrenk was a lean, spidery man, making up in height what he lacked in width. A black yarmulke perched precariously atop a thatch of iron grey hair and Jones wondered whether he used a bobbi-pin to keep the cap from falling off. His face belied his hair, looking a generation younger. A pair of magnifying goggles hung on a strap around his scrawny neck and caught the ashes from the cigarette tucked in the corner of his mouth.

Shrenk was sitting on a tall stool behind his counter picking at the insides of a cuckoo clock with dainty watchmaker's tools. "What can I do for you, my friend?" he said without looking up from his work. His accent was middle European.

Jones held out the key to Rocco's Nash. "Did you make this?"

He took the key between his thumb and forefinger, tweezer-like, and held it up to the light. His threadbare shirt cuff fell back from his wrist, and Jones saw the blue numbers tattooed on his forearm. Six numerals. Auschwitz?

"I may have. I don't stamp my keys with an initial die like Matthews.

She stamps hers with a letter M. This is a standard blank. Based on the shoulder and the octagonal bow, I'd say it's for a Nash. He looked at the grooves between the teeth. Oh yes, this is my work. He turned the edge of the key for Jones to look. "I polish the valleys between the peaks. Others don't bother. I take pride in my work."

"When you make car keys for a customer, do you make an extra set to keep on hand in case he loses them?"

"We have moved past the point where I answer questions without knowing who you are and why you ask them."

Jones shrugged. "My name is C.O. Jones. You and I have an employer in common, Skitch Mottola."

The locksmith nodded. "That is who. Now, why, C.O. Jones?"

"Let's say I'm just helping Skitch out with a little problem."

"Then I will answer your question." Shrenk gave Jones a humorless smile that stretched his thin lips taut. "I barely make a living as it is. Key blanks cost money. I couldn't afford to make extra copies of everything I do. Besides, if someone's car were stolen, the police would come here first with a warrant. Does that answer your question?"

Jones nodded. "Yes. And while I'm here, I need to buy a padlock. How much are those?" He pointed to a row of them in a display case below the counter. All had the name Wahler on their sides, the same lock he found guarding the load of heroin.

"Those are a dollar and ten cents." Shrenk pointed to a row above them. "For another sixty cents, you can have one of those Yales. Much better quality."

"No thanks, I'll take one of the Wahlers," Jones said. He pulled a dollar bill from his wallet and a dime from his pocket and laid them on the counter. Shrenk took the second lock from the right end from the case and handed it to Jones. "Keep it oiled, Mister Jones. Wahlers can be fussy. Many of their components are made with steel instead of brass, and rust can clog their works."

"I'll keep that in mind."

When Jones walked out of Shrenk's shop, he found a black and white Brownsville Police car parked behind the roadster and a uniformed patrolman in a peaked cap leaning against the Mercury's door, one foot on the running board. The cop was young, no more than twenty-five, but his eyes were a lot older. He'd seen some action overseas.

"Afternoon, officer." Jones looked pointedly at the parking meter. He still had eight minutes left.

The cop straightened up and took a step toward Jones. He was about the same height and weight, but his long arms gave him an inch or two more reach.

A pair of grey eyes over a long straight nose locked with his. Jones recognized the family resemblance. He was Jenny Matthews' brother, or at least her cousin. A braided lanyard attached his service revolver to the epaulet on his right shoulder. On his left hand, instead of a wedding band, Jones spotted a heavy silver Navy ring on the cop's finger.

"I hear you found a car key." His voice was a little bit high and nasal for a guy his size.

"Word gets around fast. Did you lose one?"

The cop's eyes narrowed. "We don't believe in 'finders keepers' around here, pal. You find something, you turn it in to the police."

"Meaning you." Jones grinned. "That was snappy detective work, knowing where I'd go next." He took a step forward, but the cop stood his ground. "If there's a reward, I want it. I tell you what, Officer—"

"Colton."

"Officer Colton." Jones shook a Lucky halfway out of the pack and pulled it the rest of the way with his teeth. He talked around it. "I think I'll just hang onto the key for now. If somebody's car turns up missing," he twitched his head to the back of the Mercury, "you already have my license number, a diligent fellow like you. And I'll bet your sister even told you my name, didn't she?"

Colton blinked. The question caught him off guard. "Uh–"

"Give her a message for me. Tell her that C.O. Jones told you Max Shrenk wouldn't say whose key it was either," he lied.

Jones walked around the front of the roadster and opened the passenger door. "I'll sleep better tonight knowing you're on duty, Officer Colton." He slid across the seat and under the steering wheel. Jones started the car and pulled away from the curb.

Colton still had not moved.

XXIII

Jones drove back to the pool room, keeping an eye on the rearview mirror. If Colton tailed him, he was better than average. Of course, trying to tail anybody in a marked police car was outright stupid, and Colton

"I'll sleep better tonight knowing you're on duty, Officer Colton."

didn't look that dumb. Jones almost wished he would have followed him to the pool room and realized who he worked for. If he were on the pad like other town cops, Colton would lay off. But, Jones thought, he'll figure it out soon enough.

Then there was his sister Jenny, attractive but hard-edged. Different last name, probably married. She didn't wear a wedding ring, but plenty of people who work with their hands don't. Shrenk didn't wear one either. Maybe she works the shop with her husband, he thought.

Neither of the locksmiths really gave Jones anything he didn't already know. Shrenk admitted making the spare key for Rocco's Nash. His shop had the Wahler padlocks, but Jones figured that he could find them in any hardware store. As for Jenny Matthews, she and her cop brother were worth another look. If Colton's on the take, he thought, she might be in on it too, and willing to cash in on an opportunity.

Jones parked down the street past the spots reserved for Skitch and his crew. Three of the four were occupied; Skitch's Buick, Jack Mozzo's Cadillac, and Dodie's cherry red convertible. Herman, the black man who ran a shoe shine stand in the pool room was busy polishing Mozzo's car with a rag. Herman wore the Purple Heart he earned on D-Day pinned to the front of his jacket.

"Afternoon, Herman. How's tricks?"

"Another day another supper, Jones." Herman had called Jones 'Mister' the first time they spoke, and Jones told him, "Just Jones, Herman. Save Mister for people who need to feel big. I'm just another vet."

Herman looked down the street at the Mercury. "You got you new wheels, huh?"

Jones shook his head. "Just a loaner, Herman. Ford's in the shop."

"Fillin' up them holes I saw in the fender, eh?" He cackled. "Bet the wind whistle through them like a flute."

"You got that right. Makes it hard to sneak up on people."

Herman laughed and went back to shining Mozzo's Cadillac.

The gym was less busy than usual that day. As Jones waited for the elevator, he saw Danny come out of the locker room in his street clothes. He waved and kept on walking for the stairs. No news.

As the elevator passed the third floor, Jones saw a half dozen men clustered around the craps table. The shooter, a thickset man in a suit a half-size too small for him threw the dice. He raised his fists in triumph and the other players groaned. An amateur, thought Jones. A pro wouldn't even smile. He's got the fever. Whatever he won on that throw, he'll lose on the next two.

The fourth floor was hectic. Men in shirtsleeves were bustling around the long tables where the "policy" slips were organized for the numbers game. One table had a bigger pile than most.

"What's with the tall pile?" Jones asked Buckshot. "Somebody get a hot tip?"

"Four-thirty-seven," the bodyguard replied. "Word's out it'll hit today."

The winning number was determined by the last three digits of the day's end balance of the U.S. Treasury, something seemingly impossible to rig. But, Jones thought, for every lock a human can invent, some sonofabitch will find a way to open it.

Skitch was standing behind his desk gazing at the painting of Florence. "Some day, I want to go there, take Frankie with me and let him see what his roots are."

"Florence?"

"Nah, not just Florence, Italy. All of it, so he appreciates where all this began." Skitch pulled his chair away from the desk. "Sit down, sit down," he said, waving to a chair on the other side. "Some Johnny Bull made a crack to me once about being a Dago; you know what I said? I said, 'Just remember while my ancestors were having orgies, yours were out grubbing around in the woods looking for a root to gnaw on.'"

Jones laughed. "Sounds accurate."

Skitch's smile dropped off his face. "So, what have you found out?"

"That there are more questions in this town than answers."

Skitch took a cigarette from the box on his desk and offered one to Jones. "I guess for an outsider that's accurate too. People who spend their whole lives in Brownsville take a lot of things for granted. What can I tell you?"

"Shrenk."

"The Jew. What about him?"

"How long has he been here?"

"Came to Brownsville right after the war was over. The Krauts had him in a concentration camp. He just sort of fell into place. He gave some competition to Matthews for the first time in a long time."

"Must pay well for him to have a new Chevy in his garage."

"There's an example of what you don't know about hometown life, Jones. The Jewish community sticks together here, and when one of their people arrives from the old country, they all chip in to loan him money to start a business and give him a car so he can get around. From that point, he either sinks or swims. If we didn't keep Shrenk on retainer, he'd probably starve to death."

"How about Jenny Matthews and her brother the cop?"

"You have had a busy day, haven't you?" Skitch leaned back in his chair. "Roger Matthews, Jenny's husband ran the lock shop. He got drafted. She took over the business when he shipped out. He was killed in combat someplace in France. She still runs the place, and she does a good job of it."

"And the brother?"

"Rudy Colton." Skitch frowned. "He came back from the war with a chip on his shoulder. He's a tough cop; doesn't take any shit from the locals, likes to bust heads a little too much, but he plays ball."

"You mean he's on the pad?"

Skitch nodded. "But I don't think he likes it much."

Jones told him of his conversation with Jenny and his encounter with Colton. "She had him on my ass as soon as I drove away."

"He's protective of her, that's for sure. A lot of the hometown guys would like to take her out, but Colton scares them away."

"Life in a small town."

"So tell me, Jones, out of curiosity, why did you ask Jenny and Max different questions?"

"I already knew Shrenk made the key for Rocco. He was cagey with me but cooperated once I said I was working for you. Jenny Matthews was confrontational from the word Go. I wanted to see how she'd handle something that looked shady."

"And she called her brother."

Someone knocked at the door. Dodie came in. He was wearing a teal blue shirt today. "Just came over the wire. Four-thirty-seven's the number."

"Won't that take a big bite?" Jones said, "I saw the pile of slips outside."

Skitch shook his head. "Nah. We had shills bet big on the number with other operations; our boys kick back eighty percent to us. It offsets the nickel and dime civilian winnings."

"So you knew that number would hit."

Skitch shrugged. "We started the rumor. It's good for business to let the everyday Joe win once in a while, or eventually, they'd give up and we'd have to find some other way to make money."

"Every day's an education around here."

"It ain't L.A. That's for sure."

"Amen."

"Got a fin in your wallet, Jones?"

"Probably."

"Wanna play poker? Best hand from the serial number wins. As and ones are aces, zeros are tens."

Jones chuckled. "Why do I think I'm gonna lose?"

"Tell you what. So you know there's no trick, I'll open my wallet, and you can pick out the bill, just so you know the game isn't rigged."

"Okay." He turned to Dodie. "You in?"

"Sure. Winner take all." He reached for his wallet, and Skitch pulled an alligator billfold from his hip pocket. He opened it and Jones thumbed through it 'til he found a five. Dodie opened his wallet and let Jones choose a bill. "Your turn."

Jones had two fives in his money clip. He let Dodie pick one sight unseen. "That one'll do."

Skitch laid the bills out left to right face down, Dodie's, Jones's and his own. "Read 'em and weep," he said. He turned over Dodie's bill. The serial number was A37582103N. "Pair of treys." Jones's number was K66309146B. "Three of a kind. Good hand, Jones." He wiped his brow with the back of his hand. "You got me sweating."

Jones appreciated the theater. As Skitch turned his own bill over, the Sight showed Jones the number: J37049318R. "Jack-high straight." Skitch swept the bills from the desk and tucked them into the pocket of his vest. "Double or nothing? Play with tens?"

"Once bitten," said Jones. "So tell me, how did you get me to choose the winning bill from your wallet?"

Skitch and Dodie looked at each other. Dodie shrugged. "He won't tell."

"I'm surprised an ex-carny like you doesn't know the gaffe." Skitch took the remaining fives from his wallet and fanned them out on the desk. Jones looked over the serial numbers. Nothing offered less than a full house.

Skitch reached into the inside pocket of his suit coat and pulled out a long billfold. He threw it on the desk. "That's my real wallet. A lot of money passes through here. I go through the take every now and then and if I find a bill with a good hand on it, no matter what the denomination, I put it in this one." He tapped the alligator billfold. "It didn't matter which bill you chose; they're all winners. Maybe someday I'll lose, but I haven't yet."

"Like I said, Skitch, every day's an education."

XXIV

The next morning, Jones walked into Fiddle's, his newspaper under his arm. Jenny was sitting alone in a booth near the back of the diner. She was almost done with a plate of bacon and cottage fries, a pack of cigarettes beside her coffee cup.

Her hair was wound into a tight bun on the back of her head, and instead of the grey shop coat, she wore a tan suede jacket over a dark blue blouse. Jenny looked up as Jones approached the booth.

"I met your brother." No response but a cold look from the stone grey eyes. "Did he give you my message?" Still no answer. Jones smiled and gestured to the empty side of the booth. "May I join you?"

"No."

"She speaks."

"Buzz off, okay? Let me eat my breakfast in peace."

"Sure," Jones said. "Just one question."

"What?"

"Doesn't pulling your hair back like that make your teeth hurt?"

In spite of herself, Jenny chuckled. She shook a Chesterfield out of the pack and before she could find the book of matches in her pocket, Jones had his lighter out. She hesitated for a second then leaned in to light her cigarette on its flame. She held the cigarette between her index and middle fingers but with the lit end pointed into her palm so that when she took a drag on it, her lips would brush her knuckles.

"You're quick on the draw, Jones."

"Better quick than slow."

Mabel came over with the coffee pot and a cup on a saucer. She stood looking back and forth between Jenny and Jones, unsure whether to put the cup on the table.

"Oh hell," said Jenny, flicking an ash onto her saucer. "Sit down."

Jones slid into the booth opposite Jenny and Mabel poured his coffee. "The usual, Jones?"

"Yeah, and put her breakfast on my tab." Mabel topped off Jenny's cup and hustled off to the kitchen with the order. Jenny poured cream into the cup and stirred it with her spoon.

Jones took a sip of his coffee and set down the cup. "I like the coffee here. For me, it's no good unless it climbs out of the cup and comes after me."

"Stronger than I make it."

"*De gustibus non est disputandum.*"

"What?"

"It's Latin. It means more or less that there's no disputing taste."

"So you're either an educated thug or a defrocked priest. I'm guessing thug. My brother says you work for Skitch Mottola."

Jones nodded assent. "Does that change anything between us?"

"No. All the more reason to not trust you."

"But at least I'm working for the home team."

Jenny's hand twitched and bumped her coffee cup, making it rattle on the saucer. It was just enough for Jones to see he'd struck a nerve.

"I guess your brother keeps you up on community news."

She took a long drag on her cigarette, swallowed the smoke and let it out in a long slow stream. "I hear things."

Jones knew better than to push. "So how did you become a Lockie?"

"My husband Roy took over the shop when his father died. I worked with him and learned the trade by doing, just like he did. Then Roy went overseas and he died. It's a common story."

"You don't seem bitter."

"It's life, Jones." She stubbed out her cigarette in the saucer. "It's life in this town. Thanks for breakfast." She slid from the booth and stood.

"You're welcome," Jones said. "See you around."

"Hard not to in a town this size." She turned as she was about to walk away. "Oh, and to answer your question, the bun doesn't make my teeth hurt, but it can be hell on my scalp."

She walked away, and Jones watched her in the mirror behind the counter as she went out the door.

Mabel set down Jones's plate. "She a tough one, for a woman."

Jones smiled. "I don't think being a woman has anything to do with it."

XXV

The day was uneventful. Danny spent most of his time at the gym watching for Collins and Mateosky, and Jones spent most of his time sitting on the bench across the street from the pool room reading *A Connecticut Yankee in King Arthur's Court* and watching for anybody passing by who looked as if he may be watching the pool room.

In the middle of the afternoon, Danny came out and sat beside Jones. "Anything?"

Jones shook his head. "Business as usual." He looked up and down the street. "The same cars have been parked in the same spaces for the last two hours, all but that tan Ford up the block. It's been there all day with nobody in it."

"Same upstairs. Nothing out of the ordinary. It's too quiet. What's that saying, the calm before the storm?"

"Yeah. That about sums it up."

"The reason I came out is that Skitch wants to see you upstairs. I'll watch the street."

Jones dog-eared the page he was reading and stood up, stretching. "I'll be right back."

The pool room was half empty, but that was ordinary until after four o'clock when the shifts changed. The gym was half empty too, a few people working the bags and lifting weights. From ringside, Fats Mungo was bellowing at Billy French and Red Jefferson. "Head down, French! Head down! You want him to knock it off? Keep those elbows in, Red, goddamnit! You'd kill each other if you weren't so goddamned lame!"

The elevator cage opened, and Buckshot took him upstairs. Jones noticed a bulge under his jacket he hadn't seen before. A pistol in a shoulder rig, thought Jones. It may be quiet, but Skitch is taking things seriously.

In the office, Skitch was on the phone, so Jones waited outside the door until he hung up. Dodie was in one of the chairs, so Jones sat in the other.

"Jesus, Mary, and Joseph," Skitch said.

"Trouble?" Jones said.

"Could be. Some reporter from *Colliers Magazine* has been nosing around undercover, and the magazine's about to publish a big exposé on the Mob in Western Pennsylvania. Mentions me by name; maybe I oughta be flattered."

"No news people don't know already," Dodie said.

"You think it's connected to the current situation?" Jones asked. "The timing seems too good to be a coincidence."

"Yeah, I thought of that," Skitch said, "and so has New Kensington. You think this outfit sicced the reporters on us to make us pariahs?"

"If it helps to alienate you from new Ken, it would be a viable tactic. This game looks more sophisticated every day."

"Well, this time it won't work. New York sent some boys to strong arm the publisher, and he postponed the story indefinitely."

"Whoever's running this show has some reach and some imagination." Jones said.

"Enough about that. The reason I called you in, I need you to run an errand for me. Tonight around eleven, I need you to go to the High Point. Remember Smitty?"

"The bag man? Little guy with thick glasses?"

Skitch nodded. "He's bringing a briefcase to the High Point to hand off to you; no cash, just ledgers. I want to go over the books. For all I know, if somebody from the outside's angling for a takeover, I need to make sure he isn't tapping our money along with everything else he's got going."

"Makes sense. Why not bring them here directly?"

"Because if somebody wants to get his hands on them, this is the place they know they can go for it. I want to see some mug try to grab them from you. Take Hayes along, and bring the ledgers back here."

"No problem."

"Don't say that," Dodie said. "You might jinx yourself."

"Glad I'm not superstitious," Jones said. "But I'll keep it in mind in the future."

"Jones," said Skitch, "you got any money on the Charles-Valentino fight tonight?"

"I'm not much for betting on other people. I'd rather bet on myself; that way I have more say in how it turns out."

XXVI

"I don't see Smitty's car," Danny Hayes said, as Jones pulled the Mercury into the gravel parking lot of the High Point. The local watering hole perched at the top of a wooded bluff, steep enough to be called a cliff by many, overlooking a horseshoe bend in the Monongahela River. Local river pilots called it the "Hell Stretch" because of the difficulty of navigating a string of coal barges around the curve.

"We're early."

The High Point was a roadhouse built like a tunnel on the narrow strip of land between the highway and the edge of the cliff, affording a spectacular view of the river valley below. It was a low-budget gathering place for blue-collar workers and their wives and sweethearts, packed on the weekends when a trio provided live music for dancing. Tonight, Jones counted eight cars in the parking lot beside the bar and three in the gravel lot across the road. Two years before, the same lots were full when Jones shot it out with a carload of hired guns. *I was moving a satchel that night too*, Jones recalled. What goes around, comes around.

Music blared from the jukebox inside as he stepped out of the roadster. Spike Jones and His City Slickers — no relation. In fact, Jones didn't believe he had any living relations on the planet. The frenetic music, punctuated with bells, slide whistles, and fog horns, seemed out of place in an empty bar. Danny put on his jacket but didn't bother to zip it shut. "Can't see my breath in the air yet, but it's gonna be cold tonight." The Western Pennsylvania Indian Summer had faded away two days before.

Jones pulled his pack of Lucky Strikes from a pocket and lit one with a wooden match. He blew a lungful of smoke and watched it spread in slow motion in the crisp Autumn night, tinted by the neon lights that ran across the roofline of the bar. "Let's go in. Smitty'll show soon enough. It's cold out here already."

"Your blood's still tuned to L.A. weather," Danny jibed. "And so's your wardrobe. You'll need a warmer coat in a couple of weeks."

Jones zipped his waist-length jacket to his chin and pulled his lat lower on his forehead.

Tonight's job was simple. Show up to pick up a bag from Michael "Smitty" Smitolli and take it back to the pool room in Brownsville where he would deliver the satchel to Skitch; no money, just the ledgers.

Jones opened one of the double doors at the entranceway and the music got louder. The High Point was arranged like a shotgun shack with the kitchen and bar at one end and booths and a small dance floor at the other. Overhead, in a whimsical moment, someone had painted a blue sky and cottony clouds on the ceiling.

Lou was tending bar with Margie, his wife, working the booths. The cook was gone for the night. Gino Scalise, the owner was on his last legs from cancer, Jones had been told, but he hadn't been around much anyway since the gun battle two years before when a turncoat put a bullet into Gino Junior.

The vacant bandstand stood in shadow, and most of the light in the place came from neon lights behind the bar. Weeknights were usually slow as a Temperance meeting on New Year's Eve at the High Point, and this Tuesday was no exception. Danny and Jones sat at the far end of the bar, waiting for Smitty to show up.

The clock tipped toward one a.m., and most of the scanty clientele was

gone. Two guys sat at the other end of the bar, three men dirty from shov-
eling coke were shooting pool at the table near the kitchen, and some guy
in a cheap green suit sat with two frowsy women at a booth, talking loud-
ly enough to compete with the jukebox. The pool shooters finished their
game, drank up, and walked out.

Jones leaned over and said quietly. "Those two at the other end are
stone sober, and they've been here longer than we have."

Danny stole a quick look at the pair in the mirror behind the bar. Both
were dressed in work clothes. One, a tall, rangy man with a chin like a
cowcatcher had a snap-brim cap pulled low over his forehead. The other
was short and thick, hatless, showing off a close-cropped head of blonde
hair with a jagged pink scar running across the left temple.

"What do you think?'"

"I think they aren't drinking at all. There's a puddle on the floor between them. They're pouring it out." Jones called Margie over. She was a
dye-job redhead, and like Lou, she was pushing fifty and fighting gravity.
Margie leaned in, and Jones said, "Laugh."

She blinked. "What?"

"Laugh. Just do it." He handed her a nickel.

Margie giggled, and Jones leaned in to whisper in her ear. "Go outside to
the phone booth in the parking lot and call the phone in here. Ask for me."

Margie started to laugh again and saw the look on Jones's face. His
mouth was smiling but his eyes weren't. "Okay, Jones, you got it." She
walked away.

Danny observed, "Neither one of them looks like he's carrying, unless
it's a mighty small piece."

The guy in the green suit and his girlfriends finished their drinks and
got up to leave. They were heading for the door. Jones raised two fingers.
"Hey, Lou."

The bartender read the signal and came over, Jones said under the music, "Bring us a couple of drafts and go lock the back door."

Margie walked out behind the tipsy trio. Lou came back in a minute
with two beers and nodded to Jones. The phone rang. Lou picked it up. He
listened for a second then looked around and spoke to the room at large as
if he didn't know them. "Anybody here named Jones?"

"I'm Jones."

"For you."

Jones went behind the bar and put the handset to his ear. "Yeah."

Margie's voice was hushed. "There are four guys hanging around outside near the front doors. One of them's looking in the windows."

"Okay, Margie. Go to my car, the green roadster. Stand behind it. Stay put."

"What's going on?"

"Just do what I tell you." He hung up. "Thanks, Lou." He turned away from the pair down the bar and his voice dropped. "Stay out of the way." Jones went back to his stool.

He turned to Danny. "Go to the can, and when you pass the entrance doors, throw the bolt at the top of one door or the other. There are four men outside. I'm guessing they're waiting for some signal from those two. When you come back, grab a pool cue. I'll take the two at the bar, you hold off whoever comes through the door. Put down the first one and the rest'll trip over him. Don't shoot anybody unless you have to."

The last platter on the juke box slid back into the rack and the place went quiet. Danny nodded. He stood, downed his shot, and said, "Time to piss. Don't drink my beer or I'll kick your ass."

Jones laughed. "Sure you will." Down the bar, the short guy rolled up his sleeves.

Showtime.

"Okay, fellows," Lou announced. "Everybody drink up. We're closing."

The short man stood and slapped a fifty-dollar bill on the bar. "Fifty bucks says you can't throw us out of here." The voice was nasal and the accent pure Arkansas cracker.

"I'll take that bet." The men turned and eyed Jones. He was still sitting on his stool, but he had swiveled to face down the bar.

"Oh yeah?" The tall one slithered off his stool to stand beside his partner. "Who are you?"

"Does it matter?"

"Hell, no." The Hat Man slid brass knuckles onto his left hand then took off his cap and set it on the bar.

The signal.

A lot of things happened at once. The pair at the bar rushed Jones at the same time the four outsiders started through the entranceway. They had planned to come through both doors, and when they found the right one locked, the first man charged through the other side. Danny stood just outside his line of vision and swung the pool cue like a Louisville Slugger, catching the thug across his eyebrows. His knees buckled and he fell back into the doorway, colliding with the man behind him, who stumbled over his friend into the room, leaning forward. Danny brought the cue down hard across the back of his head.

The bar thugs tried to flank Jones, but he slipped a punch from Shorty and cross kicked his knee. Shorty didn't go down, but he wavered enough that he couldn't sidestep Jones's right to his jaw that put him on his back. The Sight showed him the punch that was coming. He jerked his head back as the brass knuckles swished past his chin. Hat Man had made the mistake of putting them on where Jones could see them. It was an intimidation tactic, but it told Jones the man was a lefty. He played to it, coming from Hat Man's left side so his long punches would come from his right instead.

With a crash of glass and splintering wood, one of the outsiders burst through the panels of the locked door. At the same time, the fourth of the invaders grabbed at the cue, trying to wrestle it from Danny. The guy outweighed Danny by a good thirty pounds, but trying to take a pugil stick from a Marine is a losing proposition. The thug tried to twist it from Danny's grip, and instead of pulling back, Danny shoved it under his chin into his larynx.

As the man fell away clutching his throat, his partner brought a piece of pipe down, missing Danny's head but hammering his shoulder. Danny felt his arm go numb as he danced away. His opponent leered at him through the blood from a dozen glass cuts on his face.

Hat Man did exactly what Jones wanted him to do. He tried a short jab at Jones with his armored left, and Jones sidestepped the punch. He caught Hat Man's wrist with his left hand, twisting the wrist and pulling him forward, at the same time landing a vicious blow just under his ear.

Hat Man sagged to the floor, but before he hit, Shorty was on the attack again. He grabbed Jones sideways in a bear hug, pinning his outside arm to his side. The gorilla was strong enough that he would have broken some of Jones's ribs if the arm hadn't gotten in the way.

Jones drove his free elbow into Shorty's eye. Once, twice, and on the third blow, Shorty's grip relaxed enough that Jones could twist free. Shorty caught Jones under his eye, and Jones came back with a combination of lefts and rights that drove the blond man down.

Danny was losing ground to the man with the pipe, blocking the weapon but barely able to hold onto the cue stick with both hands as he fended off the blows. The thug swung his bludgeon like he might swing a machete cutting brush, from the left, then from the right, beating Danny back. Danny caught on to the rhythm, and anticipating the next blow, twisted his torso, shortened his grip on the stick, and drove it lengthwise into his opponent's crotch. The man screamed, dropped the pipe, and grabbed at his jewels. Danny swung the cue one more time, and knocked him out.

Jones pulled the brass knuckles off Hat Man's hand and hefted them. "You okay?" he asked Danny.

"Yeah," Danny said, trying to rub feeling back into his arm," but it'll be a few minutes before I can do that again."

"Lou." The bartender stood up behind the bar clutching a sawed-off shotgun. "Call Skitch. Tell him what happened." Jones stepped over the men in the doorway and out into the parking lot. The man with the aching throat had pulled himself onto his hands and knees. Danny gave him a nasty kick in the head, and he fell over on his side.

"Margie?" Jones called out. He saw her head rise over the hood of the roadster. "It's okay. You can come back in now."

"I don't know if I want to."

"Suit yourself, but I don't think you want to see what happens next."

Jones went back into the High Point. Danny was going through the crew's pockets. "No I.D.s Nothing but some folding money, and not much of that."

"Weapons?"

"A few saps and knives but no guns."

"I figure you'll find the guns in their car. They wanted to make it look like a garden variety bar fight in case the cops showed up. They didn't know us from the Man in the Moon. I don't think they're here for Smitty. Could be they didn't even know he was coming. I think they just came to wreck the place."

"Bad timing. I did notice one thing, though." Hayes pointed at Shorty. "That one's got an Airborne Ranger tattoo on his forearm." He held out his palm. "I found this on one of the guys in the doorway. It's a Navy ring."

"So some of them are vets."

"From their looks, I'd bet all of them are vets. What the hell's going on?"

"I don't know, Danny, but I damn sure plan to find out."

"Holy shit."

Jones and Danny turned to find Smitty peering through the shattered door. His eyes were huge behind his wire-rimmed glasses. Behind him, Nick Tomasi, his driver, stood, holding a pistol.

"Just in time, Smitty," Jones said. "Give us a hand."

The four dragged the unconscious hoods outside and piled them into their car, a new Hudson Terraplane parked across the road. Jones opened the trunk and reached in. "Look what we have here." He handed Danny a rifle.

"M-1," Danny said.

"Two more just like it, and this little beauty." Jones slid a pistol from a holster. "Two-inch barrel, dull finish, plastic grips. It's a Colt Junior Commando." He reached in again. "And how about this." He held up a fragmentation grenade. "These guys have military hardware."

"So what now?" Danny said.

"Bring your car around, Smitty."

"What are you going to do?"

"Teach them a lesson, Danny." Jones opened the door of the Hudson and reached inside. He pulled the gearshift into neutral and released the hand brake. "C'mon." He and Nick and Smitty got behind the car and pushed it into the road facing the cliff. Nick brought Smitty's Packard around and went bumper to bumper against the Terraplane.

Jones reached into the back window of the Hudson. Shorty was in the middle, his head lolled to the side. Jones pinched his earlobe between his thumbnail and forefinger and twisted it until the man came yowling awake.

Jones turned Shorty's head so that he could look him in the eye. "Welcome to Pennsylvania. You get one chance. Who sent you?"

"Kiss my ass," Shorty hissed.

"That's what I thought you'd say."

He waved Nick on, and the wheel man pushed the Hudson forward with his car. Metal groaned, gears ground, and the Chevy spun its wheels in the gravel for a few seconds until it got traction. The Hudson hit the fence at the edge of the drop off at about twenty miles an hour. The heavy car snapped the boards like balsa wood. Realizing what was coming, Shorty tried to claw his way over the seat to get at the brake, the steering wheel, anything to stop the car, but his friends were in his way.

The Hudson broke through the fence, and Shorty screamed as it tipped over the edge of the bluff. Nick slid the Chevy to a halt in the gravel, its front bumper just over the edge. The Terraplane crashed downward through the trees and brush with the snapping of branches and the breaking of glass.

"Too bad," Danny said, lighting a cigarette. "That was a nice car."

"I bet they'll let you have it cheap," Smitty said.

"How far down is it to the river?" Jones asked.

"About three hundred feet, right, Danny?" Hayes nodded.

"How far do you think they got?"

"Maybe halfway."

"They'll be back, won't they?" Smitty said.

Jones nodded. "And more like them."

The Hudson snapped the boards like balsa wood.

XXVII

Jones and Danny followed Smitty into Brownsville and to Snowdon Square. The shades were pulled on the big windows facing the street, but light bled around the edges.

Nick stayed on the street to watch the cars. Smitty got to the door first, a leather satchel in his hand and by the time Danny and Jones got to the stoop, Buckshot was unlocking the door. As he passed him, Jones saw the pistol in Buckshot's hand behind the door. Nobody was taking chances.

The empty pool room was eerie in the late night quiet. The tables were covered with canvas sheets like a rich man's town house vacated for the summer, and the cues were all ranked in their racks like carbines in an armory. The row of platform spectator chairs lined the back wall of the room, empty now, like the seats of a tribunal, or maybe the Inquisition.

They followed Buckshot up the stairs to the second floor. The gym was silent and dark. At the rear of the room, the elevator cage was waiting to take them to the upper floors and Skitch's office. As they stepped off the elevator on the fourth floor, Jones saw the rectangle of light from the open door of Skitch's office. "C'mon." Buckshot led the way through the maze of tables piled with policy slips.

Skitch sat at his desk, tilted back in his chair. Smoke from a cigarette hooked in the corner of his mouth drifted toward the ceiling. "So, all of you guys all right?" Skitch always asked about his men first and the money second; maybe it's just p.r., thought Jones, or maybe he really does care. His suit coat hung from the back of his chair, but Skitch still wore his vest over a white shirt with its sleeves rolled. The blue-black midnight shadow of a beard showed around his jawline.

"So," said Skitch, "Tell me about it."

Jones looked to Danny and to Smitty. Nobody else jumped in, so he recounted the fight in the bar and the disposal of the carload of thugs. "We didn't kill anybody, but it'll be a few days before they can try that again."

Skitch nodded, approving. "You think they were after this?" He tapped the satchel on his desk.

Jones shrugged, "Maybe, but this wasn't a regular pickup, was it?"

Skitch shook his head. "No, this was set up this afternoon. I ditched the schedule because of what's happened the last couple of weeks. I call people myself a few hours ahead of time."

"Maybe somebody leaked it," Danny said.

"Not likely," Skitch replied. "I knew and Smitty knew."

"I didn't even tell Nick where we were going 'til we were on the way." Smitty said.

"One thing makes me believe this wasn't about the ledgers." Jones said.

"What's that?"

"They weren't carrying guns. You don't rob a courier with these." Jones set the brass knuckles he'd taken from the brawl on Skitch's desk. "I think that bunch was sent to wreck the High Point, hit you close to home, make you look like you can't protect your own turf. They had guns all right, but they left them in the trunk of the car."

"The guns worry me," said Danny. "They were military hardware."

"Military?" Skitch said.

Danny set the stubby Colt Commando on the desk. Its matte finish contrasted the gloss of the desk top. "Right there," Danny pointed to three letters stamped on the frame in front of the hammer. "G.H.D.," he said. "That's the acceptance mark of Brigadier General Guy H. Drewry. Under it you see the flaming bomb; that's the government ordnance acceptance stamp. This piece is military issue. The Colt Commando's still in use, so I don't think they picked it up in an Army Surplus store."

"Maybe one of these mugs brought it home as a souvenir." Skitch said.

"Along with a couple of M-1s and a frag grenade?" Jones shook his head. "Somebody with connections is arming these people."

"That worries me." Skitch stubbed out his cigarette. "Maybe next time they'll bring a bazooka."

Danny let out a long breath. "And the Airborne tattoo I saw on one of them makes me think they're ex-military, vets home from the war. Trained to do nothing but kill people and break things."

"Well, we know how to break a few things ourselves. Better that you two didn't kill them. The cops can look past a car that 'accidentally' went through a fence and over a cliff. They can't ignore dead people."

Jones spoke up. "We pretty well know now that the incidents are all part of a bigger plan. Hitting you at random already made you change your patterns. You have too many doors to watch for the men available to watch them."

Skitch nodded. "I agree. I have to think about this." He stood. "You did good work tonight. Go get some sleep."

Back at the flophouse, Jones saw the gnomish manager dozing behind the desk. He climbed the stairs slowly, listening at every step. It's too soon for revenge for tonight, he thought, but for all I know, they've been staking me out since I hit town.

When he got to the second floor landing, he reached behind him and drew the automatic from his waistband. The hallway was lit by one bare bulb in an overhead fixture whose glass globe had been broken or stolen years before. No noise, no movement. He silently picked his way along the hall, placing his feet along the baseboards where the flooring was less likely to squeak.

His room was near the middle. Jones put his right shoulder to the wall beyond the doorway and worked the key with his left hand. The lock was noiseless; Jones had oiled it liberally. The door swung outward and he aimed the pistol past the jamb while he groped for the light switch with his free hand. The light came on and a startled mouse darted under a corner of the baseboard. Otherwise, nothing and no one. Old habits die hard, thought Jones, so I don't die easy.

He closed and locked the door behind him and threw his hat on the dresser. The bed was as he left it that morning. No maid service. Jones shucked off his shirt and trousers and set his automatic on the nightstand. He thumbed off the light and stretched out on the rumpled sheets. He was asleep before the mouse had the nerve to come out of hiding.

XXVIII

Dreams came as they often did. But Jones's dreams weren't the fanciful kind; they were stark reminders of a past he'd rather have forgotten, but that wouldn't go away. Some nights he dreamt about the farm where Roy Hankins, his cruel foster father worked him and beat him like the proverbial rented mule. Other times, he dreamt about Stutter's Extravaganza, the Carnival he traveled with after he ran away from the farm.

Tonight he dreamt about the night in England after he'd destroyed the *Sylléktis* and killed Chirac. Hennessey was waiting for him in a farm house outside Exeter. He debriefed Lieutenant Simmons in under an hour, giving Simmons the impression that Hennessey knew all the details already, and his report was a simple formality.

"Do you think that the SS will try to build it again?" Simmons asked.

"They could, but it's too late."

"Too late for what?"

"That's classified, Wormwood, but I can tell you this much: in a little over a week, it won't matter. Tonight, get some rest. You've earned it."

Sleep came quickly for Simmons, who had been awake for most of three days. The overstuffed tick of the farm house bed held him like a protective hand. In the middle of the night, he bolted awake. His heart raced, and his breathing was quick. He felt the itch of his tattoos and threw back the comforter to see them glowing a dull red in the darkness.

Then he looked toward the ceiling and saw the eyes. If they had had a face, it would have filled the whole ceiling of the room. They were the eyes he saw in Paris staring down from the apex of the *Sylléktis*. Simmons couldn't move, couldn't look away as they bored into him. Then as he watched, they faded.

Shaken, Simmons sat on the edge of the bed and fumbled a cigarette out of the pack. He was halfway through it when Montrose, one of Hennessey's British Commando liaisons burst into the room, a Sten machine gun in his hands.

"Get dressed. We're leaving. Something's wrong outside." He disappeared into the corridor.

Simmons was halfway dressed when he heard gunfire and screams, the bark and snarl of the mastiff guard dog and its hideous howl of pain. His tattoos were a dull yellow now, and pulsing with heat. He pulled on his boots and was tying the second one when Montrose returned. "Hurry up. Its…"

His words were cut off by a pair of hands ending in claws that reached around him from behind and plunged their fingers through his ribs. Montrose shrieked in pain and his eyes rolled back in his skull. His fingers reflexively clenched, and flame and lead shot from the barrel of the machine gun. Simmons dove to the floor as bullets sprayed the wall above him like mad embroidery.

The hands pulled apart, and with a wet ripping sound, opened Montrose's chest like the doors of an armoire. His gory entrails sagged from the gaping cavity and Simmons could see his heaving lungs and the last few pulses of his heart. The Sten clattered to the floor and Montrose's body slumped on top of it. Then Simmons saw the raw face of horror.

The invader wore British field greens, seams bursting from the eruption of bone and muscle within. The bulk of its shoulders shoved its head forward and down as if relegating the mind to secondary importance. The face was raw, distorted bone and muscle splitting the skin and making it a parody of humanity. The mouth gaped open to show ranks of teeth like the maw of a shark. Its glowing eyes were the eyes that had stared from the ceiling.

The horror raised one of its rawboned hands and extended its forefinger at Simmons. The creature spoke, but its guttural sounds only resembled words. Simmons' tattoos glowed white hot. Any second they would burst into flame.

Hennessey dove through the doorway, his fists wrapped around the handle of a bayonet. The Colonel drove the point between the monster's shoulder blades and out the other side of its bulging chest. The words turned to a roar then to a shrill keening as smoke rose from the wound and poured from the creature's nose and mouth.

It staggered around the room, smashing holes in the walls with its fists. The monster grabbed the blade protruding from its chest with both hands, trying to push it out the way it came, and the sinewy hands burst into bright yellow flame. The creature fell to its knees, raised its head to stare at Simmons with those glowing, baleful eyes, and opened its mouth to speak one last time.

A flash in the candle light, and the head fell from the body. It rolled into a corner and the eyes winked shut. Hennessey stood over the smoking corpse with a hooked Kukri knife in his hand. He wiped the blade on the tattered uniform, then pulled the smoking bayonet from the body. He held it up to the light and turned it over in his hand. "Plated with silver," Hennessey said, matter-of-factly.

"What—what was that?" Simmons blurted.

"Apparently the wizard who manipulated the *Sylléktis*. He took over the body of the guard, a kind of possession. You spoiled his show and he wanted personal revenge. Stupid. If this didn't kill him at a distance, I'm guessing it did a lot of damage." He nodded at Simmons' feet. "Tie your boot lace." Hennessey said and walked out of the room without another word.

XIX

Jones woke to the rustle of the newspaper as Marty, the paperboy slid it under his door. He paid Marty to bring the *Telegraph* every morning and slip it under the door of his room headline down. Jones told him, "I don't like to read bad news until I'm ready," but his real reason for the request was an issue of security. If the paper came through headline up, someone else put it there and was probably standing on the other side of the door with a gun, waiting for him to stoop to pick it up. The ploy had saved him once, and it might save him another day. Old habits.

He pulled on his trousers and went down the hall to the common bathroom to wash and shave. The mirror over the sink was foggy around the edges, but clear enough for Jones to make out his black eye from the night before. Jones dressed in khaki trousers and a clean chambray shirt, one of the three that hung in the open closet. He laced his boots and tucked his automatic in his waistband behind his back then put on his jacket and his hat. He folded the newspaper under his arm, and set off for Fiddle's.

It was a little bit late for breakfast, but Jones decided that the ham-and-eggs special at Fiddle's was what he wanted. In the diner a half dozen men lounged on stools drinking coffee and arguing over the Charles-Valentino fight. The booths were empty, so Jones took the one to the back that him a good view of the door and the street through the windows.

The radio behind the counter was tuned to KDKA out of Pittsburgh and as he unfolded his newspaper, Jones heard the announcer say that the next song, "Don't Cry Joe, Let Her Go" by Frank Sinatra was number one in the nation. Mabel came from behind the counter with a cup on a saucer and the coffee pot. "Rough night, Jones?" she said, eyeing the shiner under his left eye.

"Honey, I forgot to duck."

She snorted. "Isn't that what Dempsey told his wife after Gene Tunney knocked him out?"

"Yeah, but I won."

Mabel rolled her eyes. "You and Ezzard Charles. What'll you have?"

"Ham and eggs over easy, Mabel, and keep my cup full."

She scribbled the order on her pad. "You got it. How about a steak to go with that eye?"

"Maybe later."

She headed for the kitchen and Jones opened his newspaper.

The newspaper didn't mention the High Point incident; it was probably too late to make the morning edition. Besides the boxing match in California the big news was still the steel strike. The steelworkers' leader John Murray was making an appeal for public support.

Jones was halfway through his breakfast when the man in the tan suit walked into the diner. He stood just inside the doorway and looked the place over, moving only his eyes under the brim of his hat. He crossed toward Jones's booth, and Jones saw his thin moustache and the jagged, livid scar along his jaw. He strolled over to the booth and Jones set down his fork. He put his hand under the table to get to his automatic if he needed it.

The man in the suit smiled. "Easy, my friend. I'm unarmed."

"Your type is never unarmed."

He chuckled. "May I join you?"

"*Usiądź.*"

The man hesitated for a second, then smiled. "Clever, but I knew you would be. My name is Blake, Mister Jones." He sat and laid both hands palm down on the table top. "I believe we share a former employer in common, under other names, of course. I understand that you've been through a few aliases since the war. If I'm not mistaken, it was Lattimer in New Jersey before you got into trouble with the Benaducci family and came out here to Nowhereville."

He stopped talking when Mabel came over with a cup and the coffee-pot. "Coffee, mister?"

"Yes, thank you. That's all I need."

Mabel poured the coffee and went back to the counter, refilling cups for the loafers. The coffee sat steaming. Blake still hadn't moved his hands.

"So you know my pedigree. Why are you here, Blake?"

"I have a proposition for you, Mister Jones, a one-time offer, if you will. You have proven to be a distraction to my employer, and he would rather have you as an employee than an adversary."

"And who is your employer?"

"Someone who wants to remain anonymous."

"I could make you the same offer, but somehow, I doubt you'd take it."

Blake shook his head slowly. "Work for Skitch Mottola? He's small-time. He has nothing to offer that would interest me."

"Tell your boss I do business face-to-face only."

"That is unfortunate." Blake smiled, showing his teeth. "You know," he said, "if I had a knife under my hand, I could reach across the table and put it through your heart before you could pull that pistol you have in the hol-ster behind your back." His words were almost inaudible under the bustle of the diner, the patrons oblivious to the deadly dialog across the room.

"Or I could shoot you under the table with the pistol I've been aiming at you since you sat down."

"But which hand, Jones? I know which of your hands has the gun and a good idea of how it's pointed. Which of my hands has the knife? Which way would I twist to thrust? You might kill me, but I would definitely kill you."

"But you won't."

"How can you be so sure?"

"Because your anonymous employer hasn't ordered you to kill me. Yet."

"And 'yet' is the operative term, isn't it? Do you really have a pistol aimed at me under the table, Jones?"

"If that's a ploy to get me to show it to you so you can stab me while I'm moving the gun into view, it won't work. Do you really have a knife under your hand?"

Blake rose, slowly dragging his palms across the table top and never turning them over. "Finish your breakfast before it gets cold." He smiled again. "Another time, Jones."

"Count on it."

Jones watched Blake as he left Fiddle's and followed the hit man with his eyes until he disappeared around one of the pillars of the bridge. He understood that the next time he saw Blake it would be over his gun sight or the hit man's. Or both.

Blake was brazen to come in alone, or did he have back up? Jones studied the men at the counter. They were still arguing over the Ezzard Charles fight. None of them was watching him furtively in the mirror, and none had come in after he sat down. He slid the automatic inside the folded newspaper beside his plate and finished his ham and eggs.

XXX

When Jones walked into the pool room, Danny was waiting for him.

"I drove past the High Point a while ago. The Hudson's gone, and the fence looks like nothing ever went through it."

"Our guys?"

He shook his head. "Skitch and Dodie say no. That's a puzzle."

"Maybe not. The bad guys lost one and they don't want the word getting around that they did. Whoever is behind this operation has a lot of resources. Do you have any contacts with the local National Guard?"

Danny nodded. "Sure, I know a few guys."

"Any of them a Quartermaster?"

Danny nodded.

"Could you find out what they keep on hand in the local armory in Uniontown and whether any of it came up missing lately?"

"You're thinking that's where the guys last night got their equipment?"

"Them and the bank robber. It's a possibility, but stun grenades aren't an everyday item. That's commando gear. What's the biggest National Guard headquarters around here?"

"That would be the Hunt Armory in Pittsburgh. It takes up a whole city block."

"Maybe that's where the weapons are coming from."

"Yeah, some of that stuff ain't exactly in the war souvenir category."

You haven't looked in the trunk of my car, Jones thought. "I'll be back in an hour, give or take."

"Where're you going?"

"To see if I can get some help finding our Mister Blake."

Jones was waiting at the traffic light to cross the bridge into West Brownsville when the black-and-white pulled up behind him and the spinner came on. In his rearview mirror, Jones saw Colton's louring face over the steering wheel. He turned onto a side street, pulled to the curb, and shut off the motor.

Colton got out of his car at the same time Jones climbed out of the roadster. They stood for a moment, eyeing each other. Jones put a cigarette in his mouth and lit it as Colton approached him; hand on the pommel of his nightstick.

"Better to let your fingers down alongside the handle; get a grip on it quicker that way. I'd've thought they'd teach you that in the Shore Patrol."

"Who said I was in the Shore Patrol?"

"You're wearing a Navy ring, got a lanyard on your pistol so nobody can pull it out of your hand in a fight. You're a vet on the hometown force. Doesn't take Steinmetz to figure it out."

"I'll say this once. Stay away from my sister, Jones."

The cigarette bobbed as Jones talked around it. "Using an official vehicle for personal business on the clock; I know they didn't teach you that in the SP." He dropped his cigarette on the pavement and crushed it out with the toe of his boot. "As for your sister, Colton, it's for her to say get lost, not you. Think hard before you go for that Billy."

The pair stared each other down until Jones said. "Good decision." He took a step back and opened the door of the roadster. "Since I'm not under arrest, I believe I'm free to go. And Colton—" Jones gave him a hard stare. "Don't pull me over again unless you plan to arrest me."

Colton glared at Jones as he climbed into the car and started the engine. He climbed back into the prowl car and pulled away from the curb, doing a U-turn in the street.

Jones went around the block and headed back toward the bridge. If the local cops were on the pad for Skitch, they were all on the same team. That being the case, Colton was just looking out for his sister, although from what Jones could see, she didn't need a big brother to protect her, or anyone else for that matter. Anyone who repaired guns probably had one under the counter and another one in her purse.

Jenny was attractive, but in his current situation, Jones didn't need distractions, and he didn't want to put anyone in the line of fire. The way things were headed, Jones didn't need any attachments who could be used as leverage against him. Maybe after this is all over, he thought, then shook his head.

Across the bridge, Jones waited in a line of cars as a mile-long coal train rumbled down the main street of West Brownsville. The more time Jones spent in Brownsville, the more the place felt like a Norman Rockwell version of Jersey. Made guys ran things, the cops played ball, and the townspeople were happy in the security that the devil they knew provided.

There weren't five people in town who didn't play the numbers, and the whorehouses kept hookers off the street and out of sight. Little old ladies and children were safe on the streets after dark, everybody had a job, and the only people who got hurt were the ones who upset the status quo. The townspeople were complacent. It was how things had been for as long as any of them could remember. Like a benevolent dictatorship, Jones thought, and Skitch Mottola is the man in charge. But now, someone wants it for himself, and the boat's rocking.

The caboose rolled past, and the traffic started to move. Jones turned onto the main street and followed the tail of the train a few blocks to park in front of Janos and Maria Bronski's grocery store. Jones thought the Bronskis had replaced the display window, then realized he was mistaken. The front window was still boarded over, and under the name of the store, Jones saw that someone had meticulously painted the whitewashed wood to seem as if he were looking through the glass of the old window into the store. Bins of produce retreated in perspective and a counter fronting shelves spread across the back of the room.

Behind the counter, the painted faces of Janos and Maria looked out onto the street. Janos was smiling, but Jones felt a chill when he looked into the painted eyes of Maria. Her gaze was a warning, not a welcome. Like Janus in ancient Rome, he thought, one face to greet a stranger and the other to watch him closely until he left.

As he was about to enter the store, the door opened and a young woman came out with a paper sack of groceries in one arm and an infant in the other. Jones stepped back to let her pass, and found himself staring into the piercing eyes of Maria Bronski, who had opened the door for the young mother.

"Mister Jones." She stepped back a foot and waved him into the store. "I was wondering when you would be back."

Jones felt his tattoos begin to warm. He waved a hand toward the window. "You've done a terrific job painting the front of the store. It looks almost real."

"Janos is the artist," she said. "He studied under Ladislaw Krzton in Krakow before Hitler turned the world upside down."

"With his talent, he should be painting portraits, not running a grocery store."

"This is not a town that patronizes the arts. Come inside."

Jones stepped in and immediately his nose caught the earthy odor of vegetables and the blood scent of butchered meat. The store was empty except for a dark haired young man picking through a bin of apples and putting his choices in a paper bag, and a large woman in a flowered dress watching as Janos weighed out ground beef on a white enameled scale.

"I will be with you in a moment." Maria stepped behind the counter to the cash register and waited patiently as the man with the apples poured a handful of change on the counter and picked out the right coins, sliding them away from the pile. When he had the right amount, he scooped up the rest of the coins with the same hand and dropped them into his trouser pocket.

Maria rang up the sale, thanked him, and slid the coins from the counter with one hand into the palm of the other. When the young man turned from the counter, Jones saw the cuff of his left sleeve dangling empty. Another injured vet. The town was full of them. Jones saw them on the stools of the diners and bars or sitting in twos and threes on the sidewalk benches, men shy a finger, a hand, an arm or leg. Men trying to make a complete life with most of a body. The customer smiled and nodded to Maria as he left.

Jones leaned against one of the produce bins and smoked a cigarette while he waited for the woman in the flowered dress to finish her shopping. When she left, Maria came from behind the counter and Janos followed her. "Now, Mister Jones, we are alone."

Jones nodded. "I came because I hope you can help me."

Maria cocked her head to one side, thinking it over then stared into his eyes and said, "Give me your hand."

Jones hesitated.

"What do you fear, Mister Jones? That I will see what you wish to keep hidden? If you want my help, there can be no secrets between us." She held out her hand, and Jones put his in her palm. The fingers closed gently, but Jones knew that he could not pull away from their grip until she let him go.

His tattoos throbbed, and his brain felt as if a snake slithered through its convolutions, its tongue licking at every dark corner. All the time, Maria's dark eyes bored into his. Satisfied, she let go of his hand, and Jones let out the breath he'd been holding.

"You've seen the man with the scar," she said. "Spoken with him."

"If you've seen that much, then you know that he and I are enemies. He is part of a gang that must be stopped."

"So that the powers that be in this town can continue their rule?"

"You've lived here long enough to know that this town could do much worse than Skitch Mottola."

Maria turned and said something in Polish to Janos that Jones couldn't quite hear. Janos nodded and went behind the counter to the back of the store. He returned with a rolled up piece of paper. He said in his heavy accent, "Maria did not see him well, but I saw his face through the—the..." His voice trailed off.

"Windshield," Maria offered.

Janos nodded quickly. "Yes, the windshield of his car when it came through the store." He unrolled the paper and showed Jones a detailed pencil drawing of the car and behind the glass, the face of its driver. Jones recognized him as the man in the snap brimmed cap with the lantern jaw from the High Point.

"Have you shown this to the police?"

Janos shook his head. "I was afraid that he might be with the people who run this town, and they would come back and do worse to us."

Maria said, "But now we know that these men are *najeźdźca.*"

"Invaders," Jones translated.

"Like the German swine that overran our homeland," Janos said his voice thick with emotion.

"You want to find the man with the scar," Maria said.

"He calls himself Blake," Jones said, "but that's not his real name."

"I won't need his real name, or any name to find him." Maria reached into the pocket of her dress and pulled out the bent bottle cap. "This will lead us to him."

"Us?"

"You know what I am, Mister Jones, just as I know what you are. I must go with you and lead you to this man Blake, and then when I have done my part, you will do yours."

"And I will go too," Janos said, thrusting out his chin."

Jones gave Janos a questioning look.

"Do not doubt Janos, Mister Jones. He has killed almost as many Nazis as you have. War forges strange alliances, does it not?"

"Yes, it does."

"There are things that must be done, preparations that must be made. I will call you when I am ready." Maria read the question in Jones's eyes. "Soon, Mister Jones. Soon."

The words chilled Jones, because as Maria had seen into his soul, he had a look into hers. He saw the faces of occupying soldiers rotting from their skulls, the frenzied clawing of an officer at his scalp, desperate to root out the unnamed thing that was eating its way through his brain, and a collaborator opening his mouth as centipedes cascaded from his chin like an obscene waterfall.

Jones wasn't comfortable becoming involved again with magic, but if he was going to find Blake, Maria Bronski was likely the straight line to his target.

XXXI

Jones got to Snowdon Square as the sun was setting, painting the sky a dull orange. The pool room was almost empty. A hubbub of voices echoed down the stairs.

"What's up, Bucky?"

"Big fight upstairs. Everybody went up to watch."

The gym was crowded. A gang of noisy men dressed in everything from three-piece suits to Everlast shorts were gathered around the ring where two fighters were putting on gloves. One of them was Otto "Slugger" Brackenridge, the local light-heavyweight champ. The other was a stranger, a tall, swarthy pug whose face hinted that he'd come up the hard way.

A thick shelf of scar tissue across his eyebrows meant that either he couldn't keep his guard up, or that he frequently cut himself with a razor blade hidden in his glove to bleed like crazy and throw a bout. Watching the money change hands as the bookies worked the crowd, he guessed the latter because for the most part, the rest of his face was unscarred.

Jones stayed back and eyed the onlookers, watching for anything out of line. This would be a good time for an incident, while the place was crowded and everyone was distracted. Across the gym, the elevator cage opened and Skitch and Dodie came out with Buckshot trailing behind them.

"Well, the royalty's here, so now the fight can start." Jones turned and saw Danny standing beside him.

"I know Brackenridge. Who's the other guy?"

"Fighter from Erie named Modesto D'Amato. Word is he's a diver."

"He has that look."

"His manager, that little weasel in the brown suit wanted this fight. There's some heavy betting going on. By the way, Mateosky and Collins are both here right now."

"Don't point; just tell me where to look."

"By the Red corner in grey sweats. Buzz cut hair. That's Mateosky. Other side of the ring up close in a tan jacket, slicked back hair, that's Collins."

Buckshot went ahead of Skitch and Dodie, clearing the way to ring for them. Skitch held a roll of money over his head. "I got a thousand on Brackenridge. Who wants it?" No takers. Skitch shrugged and waved his hand to get the fight rolling.

Fats Mungo climbed into the ring. He shouted in his phlegmy voice, "All right. This is an exhibition fight not a sanctioned bout. There is no consideration of standing or titles at stake." He pointed to D'Amato. "In the blue corner, weighing in at 172 pounds from Erie, Pennsylvania, Modesto D'Amato." The fighter raised one glove in the air as if he were answering a question in grade school.

The crowd jeered. One of the gawkers at ringside called out, "Shoulda named him To-mato."

The crowd laughed, and Fats went on. "In the red corner weighing in at 176 pounds, from right here in Brownsville, Slugger Brackenridge." The local champ bounced on his toes, gloves in the air to the cheers and whistles of the crowd.

"The fight will be ten two-minute rounds unless one or the other fighter cannot continue. Clean fight, boys. Shake hands and come out fighting."

On the bell, Brackenridge and D'Amato danced out of their corners. Jones could hear the punches land and the shouts of the crowd, but he wasn't watching the fighters. "You take Collins," he told Danny. "I'll watch Mateosky."

"From right here in Brownsville, Slugger Brackenridge."

Danny nodded and circled the ring to get behind Collins.

Jones stayed outside the crowd and out of Mateosky's line of vision. The burly weight lifter wasn't watching the fight, either. He was looking through the ropes to ringside where Skitch and Dodie were pressed against the ring. To his credit, Buckshot, head turning side to side, ignored the fight and watched the crowd around them.

"Go on, Slugger, kill the bum!" "Murder him!" Jones looked up and saw Brackenridge deliver a vicious combination to D'Amato's midsection that drove him against the ropes, but D'Amato bounced back, delivering a staggering blow to Brackenridge's jaw that rocked him backward. Apparently D'Amato wasn't the palooka everybody thought he was.

The bell rang to end the first round and the fighters went to their corners.

Danny had slipped through the crowd until he was right behind Collins. He caught Jones's eye and put a finger to the side of his nose. Jones nodded acknowledgement and turned his attention back to Mateosky.

The bell rang to start the second round, and both boxers plowed into each other with all the finesse of a street brawl. Punches flew, and the noise of the crowd got louder. Mateosky had hardly moved since the fight started. Jones felt the itch of the Sight, and saw Mateosky's shoulder drop as he reached behind him. Jones would have shouted a warning to Skitch, but the words would have been swallowed by the cheers and whistles.

He started shoving his way to ringside, slipping his left hand into a set of brass knuckles. "Hey, watch it, bud," a man in work clothes shouted as Jones pushed him aside. Another said, "Whattaya think you're doing?" and grabbed Jones's jacket. Jones threw an elbow into the man's face and he bowled over backward.

Mateosky's arm came from behind him with the automatic in his fist. He pushed it under the ropes and aimed it at Skitch. Jones drove the knuckles into Mateosky's kidney with his left hand and caught the gun with his right, twisting it with all his strength. Mateosky's trigger finger snapped with a loud crack, but Jones couldn't wrestle the gun from the weightlifter's grip. Mateosky's ham-sized fist shot over his forearm and Jones saw an explosion of white light when it slammed into his forehead.

Mateosky switched hands with the automatic, aimed it at Jones's chest, and pulled the trigger. The hammer fell on the empty chamber. The crowd was still pressed closely and Jones had little room to maneuver. He didn't want to shoot for fear of hitting bystanders. He knuckled Mateosky on the side of his head, and Mateosky swung the pistol at Jones, opening a cut under his eye.

Across the ring, Danny had Collins in a half Nelson, face through the ropes against the canvas. He was pressing a small revolver against Collins's neck.

"Ring the bell! Ring the bell!" Fats shouted. The bell rang stopping the fight, but no one noticed except Brackenridge and D'Amato. Everyone else was staring at the brawl on the gym floor. Jones and Mateosky were rolling over each other from the ring toward the windows, Mateosky clubbing Jones's head with the pistol and Jones punishing Mateosky's face with a fistful of brass.

Mateosky rolled on top of Jones and pushed his knee into Jones's solar plexus. Jones's hand shot out and he ground his thumb into Mateosky's eye. The weightlifter roared in pain and rolled away. As he stood up, Red Jefferson waded in behind him and delivered a hard combination to Mateosky's kidneys. Mateosky backhanded Red across the teeth with the automatic, sending the kid sprawling.

He dropped the empty automatic and picked up a fifty-pound barbell plate, raising it over his head and charging as Jones scrambled into a crouch. Jones shoved a barbell and rolled it under Mateosky's feet. The thug stumbled over it and crashed through one of the tall windows to land head first on the sidewalk below.

By this time, guns were out. Skitch and Dodie hurried over. "What the hell was that?" Skitch said.

Jones leaned through the broken window and looked down on Mateosky's body. Blood was spreading in a dark pool from his head across the sidewalk. "The end of pretending."

Jones might have been arrested if Joe Marano, the police chief hadn't been in the crowd watching the fight. The police report said "accident," and the chief wrote off Jones's participation as self-defense. The boxing match was declared a draw, and everybody got his money back. In the chaos of the moment, Collins disappeared. The town cops didn't look too hard for him, figuring that Skitch and his people would handle things. They did.

Later, Danny said, "Good thing I put Collins down early. He was smart enough to check his automatic and load bullets in the clip." He pointed to a small pile on the table. "That's all he had in his pockets; a money clip with a few bucks, cigarettes, a box of matches and a jackknife."

Jones opened the knife and ran his thumb across the edge of the blade. Sharp as a stropped razor.

"Where's Collins now?"

"The boys're holding him at the Country Club."

"Is he talking?"

"Not yet. He's pretty damned tough."

"Let's go out there," Jones said, "and see if he'll talk to us."

XXXII

Ten minutes later, Jones was turning the roadster right at the water tower that stood at the top of Beacon Hill like one of the Martian war machines from *The War of the Worlds*. The two-lane led through a set of roller coaster hills and valleys to an intersection of the highway and a double set of railroad tracks.

Jones had heard of Republic, Pennsylvania before he ever heard of Brownsville. The town, all but owned by the mob was notorious up and down the East Coast during Prohibition for bootlegging and still for its gambling, prostitution and general racketeering. The "Country Club" was a safe house outside Republic made for people on the run from the law. On the surface, it was a two-story farmhouse, complete with an elderly married couple living in it, but beneath the basement behind a steel door that dynamite wouldn't budge was a luxurious apartment with all the comforts of the Ritz, plus an escape tunnel that opened into an abandoned mine shaft.

A mile past the railroad tracks, Jones took a right onto a gravel lane through a thick stand of pine trees that blocked the light of the waning moon. A quarter mile off the highway, he saw the house.

The Country Club stood atop a grassy knoll over fields of stubble from harvested corn. A barn with a silo and a chicken coop lay twenty yards to the right. The only vehicle in sight was an old pickup truck.

"Drive up to the barn and flash your lights twice," Danny said.

Jones did as he was told, and the rickety looking barn door slid aside on a well-oiled track. A man in a long coat and fedora, one of Skitch's people, waved him inside.

In the barn Jones saw three cars. One of them was Jack the Leg's Cadillac. He shut off the engine and climbed out while Danny spoke to the sentry. He motioned for Jones to follow him.

The house was built like so many Jones had seen in Western Pennsylvania, cut block limestone, likely quarried on the property, chimney at either end, five windows across the second floor, front and back, and two ground floor windows on either side of the doorway. Twin attic dormers rose from the roof like the eyes of a frog.

They climbed the porch and the front door opened, framing them in a rectangle of light. Inside, Jones saw a smiling, white-haired woman in an apron over a gingham dress. Behind her was a stooped, balding man in overalls and a plaid flannel shirt. Perfect, thought Jones, right off the cover of the *Saturday Evening Post*.

"Hello, boys," the woman said. "Come on in."

"Hi, Nellie," said Danny. "Hello, Edgar."

The old man waved them down the hallway. "Follow me." Jones spotted the bulge of an automatic in the hip pocket of the faded overalls. As Nellie closed the door, he saw the riot gun propped behind it. Edgar led them to a door under the second story stairs. They followed him into the basement, rough stone walls coated with whitewash but grimy with decades of dust from the coal furnace that crouched in one corner, the glow through its grated door like a view through the gates of hell.

"Through there." He pointed to a crude wooden door that should have led to a root cellar. Danny pulled it open, and Jones saw a set of concrete stairs that led to a landing. He followed Danny down the stairs, and when they reached the bottom, the door swung inward.

The door featured stair step layers of steel that would take a week to cut through with a torch. It swung quietly shut behind them. They stood in what looked like the foyer of a Manhattan townhouse: carpet on the floor, a painting of a vase of roses on the wall over a pair of upholstered chairs flanking a low table with a cut glass ashtray.

Sal, Jack Mozzo's bodyguard and driver waved Jones and Danny through a doorway.

What would have been a living room in a more conventional apartment was set up like the smoking room in a men's club with a leather sofa and matching armchairs grouped around a stone fireplace. A six-seater poker table occupied one corner and a pool table the other. In the middle of the room, a painter's tarp was spread over the carpet. In its center, Collins sat tied, arms, legs, and torso to one of the card table chairs. A floor lamp with its shade removed stood beside the chair. Its bare bulb cast a harsh light on the prisoner.

His lip was split, and blood was spattered down the front of his white shirt. Jones could see by their distortion that both of his little fingers had been broken. One of his eyes was swollen shut, and the other widened when he saw Danny and Jones come into the room.

One of the leather armchairs had been dragged over from the fireplace to face Collins. Jack the Leg sat in the chair, a cigar in one hand and a bottle of Iron City in the other like a spectator at a ball game. "The guy's unsociable," Jack said. "He don't wanna talk to me."

Jones took a gravity knife from his pocket and thumbed the button. The blade slid out and Jones thrust it up the cuff of Collins' shirt. He slit the sleeve to the elbow and tore it the rest of the way to Collins' shoulder, revealing an Airborne Ranger tattoo on his bicep.

"Looks like he's in the club," Danny said.

"Okay, Collins," Jones said, grabbing a handful of the hit man's hair in his hand and turning his head to look him in the eye. "Talk to me."

"Or what?" Collins rasped. "You'll kill me? Hell, I'm dead already."

"Maybe not, if you tell me what I need to know. We can have you in Canada by sunrise."

"Just shoot me and be done with it."

"Not that easy, pal. Hey, Sal," Jones said. "There a fuse box down here?"

"Yeah, back in the kitchen."

"Go put pennies behind the fuses." Sal disappeared through the doorway and in a minute, the lamp winked out then came back on again.

Jones cracked the handle of his knife against the bare light bulb and it shattered, throwing the room into semi-darkness. He picked up the lamp with both hands and held it as he would a rifle, the prongs of the broken bulb inches from Collins' face. He touched the prongs to Collins' skin in the tender area below his nose. There was a crackle and a spark. Collins yelped and his head jerked back.

Jones touched the prongs to Collins throat with the same result, then to his ear.

"Stubborn, ain't he?" Jack said around his cigar.

"We just haven't found the right spot yet," Jones said. "Take off his shoes, Danny, and his socks."

Collins' breath was coming a little faster now, and his good eye darted around the room, as if looking desperately for escape or rescue.

"You know, Collins, or whatever your real name is, every nerve in the body has a corresponding nerve process in the feet. That's why your feet are so sensitive. He touched the prongs to the top of Collins' foot over the arch. Then he pushed the prongs between two of Collins' toes. This time Collins screamed.

"Okay, Danny, pull down his trousers."

"No, wait! No more!" Collins shouted. Then his breath became a ragged whisper. "I'll talk."

"Give me a name," Jones said. "Who sent you and Mateosky to kill Skitch Mottola?"

"I don't know."

Jones pushed the prongs between Collins' toes again. This time he held them there a while as Collins writhed in the chair. Smoke rose from his foot and the stench of charred flesh pushed aside the smell of Jack's cigar.

"Goddamnit, I don't know," Collins screamed. "Blake gets his orders from somebody up the ladder and passes them on to us. Listen, I don't know for sure, but one time I heard Blake on the phone. He told somebody to get Robertson to pull all the strings he has to. That's all I know."

"Sound familiar?" Jones asked Danny.

Danny shrugged. "Doesn't end in a vowel." he turned to Mozzo. "Ring a bell, Jack?"

Mozzo shook his head. "Not for me."

"Tell me about Blake," Jones said, bringing the prongs an inch from Collins' good eye.

Collins swallowed hard. "He's a cold bastard. Used to be an assassin for the OSS. Told us once he crawled from foxhole to foxhole in the middle of the night cutting Germans' throats with a bayonet while they were asleep. Said if he found two men in a hole, he'd kill one and let the other one wake up to find his partner dead and wonder why he wasn't."

"You weren't at the High Point. Were you in on the grocery store bit or the bank job?"

Collins shook his head a little bit faster than necessary. "No, no, that was other guys."

"Cast of thousands," Danny said. "Lots of muscle."

"You were Airborne. How about the others?"

"All the ones I know are ex-military. Blake recruited Mateosky and me, and maybe all the others too."

"So what's the big plan? A takeover?"

Collins' features hardened. "You goddamned gangsters and your goombahs–can't be drafted because you've all got records. We go and fight and you stay home and chase our women and live the lives we deserve."

Jones looked to Danny. "Should we tell him?"

"I was a Jarhead, pal." Danny rolled up his sleeve to reveal a Marine Corps tattoo. "Birdie on the Ball."

"I was in the Army Air Corps," Jones said. "What do you say about that?"

Collins stared at them and said nothing.

"Now, why the dope? Mottola's people don't peddle heroin. In fact, they run drug dealers out of Brownsville."

"That's not true!" Collins shouted. "They sell it to school kids. They get women hooked and turn them out as whores. That's why we have to kill them, to stop them from killing everything we fought to protect."

"Somebody sold you a bill of goods, pal," Mozzo said. "We don't do that shit in our hometown."

The anger went out of Collins' eyes, replaced with doubt.

"Okay, your job was to kill the Mottolas. What about the others?"

"I don't know anything but what I was told to do."

Jones believed him. He turned to Danny and Jack. "They're working as cells, sets of operatives, each with its own objective. All in separate compartments; nobody knows what the other cells are doing or even who the others are."

"Except Blake."

"Except Blake."

"I cooperated," Collins said. "You said you'd get me to Canada by morning, right?" For the first time since Jones arrived, Collins looked hopeful.

"Sure," Mozzo said, "Canada." He nodded to Sal, who walked around behind Collins' chair. Sal took off his necktie and wrapped a turn of the blue silk around each fist. He crossed his wrists and threw the loop over Collins' head.

Collins' eyes bulged as the garotte tightened. His mouth opened and closed speaking a silent protest.

Mozzo leaned forward and ground his cigar out on Collins' knee. "Nobody said alive."

Collins went into as much of a spasm as his bonds would allow. His tongue pushed through his lips. Then he was still.

Jones cut the ropes that held Collins to the chair and the body slumped onto the tarp. Sal rolled Collins up in the canvas and he and Danny carried the corpse through the door, up the stairs through the house and out to the barn.

"You surprised me, Jones," Mozzo said. "I wouldn't've thought of the lamp."

"Some days you just have to improvise, Jack."

Half way back to Brownsville, Danny said, "So what do you think is going on?"

"Somebody wants to take over Brownsville, somebody with a lot of resources. Somebody with access to military hardware. I don't think we're looking at mob people here. Like Skitch said, if New Ken or another operation wanted Brownsville, they'd come at Skitch head-on, not run some kind of spy show.

"Up to now these guys have been working hit-and-run stuff to undermine Skitch's authority. We tipped the scale last night at the High Point. Maybe they figured we're onto them, so, it's time for the hitters they have in place try to kill Skitch and Dodie. Mateosky and Collins hung around for more than a month waiting for the order. This is long-term planning."

"What next?"

"That's what worries me. We're at a disadvantage because we have locations and systems in place that are stationary targets. They don't. These guys swoop in and hit when and where nobody expects it. I told Skitch to get Tillie and Frankie out of town."

"They're on their way to Buffalo."

"How about Dodie's wife Ruby?"

"She said she's not going anywhere. All things considered, I pity anybody stupid enough to try anything with her. She carries a .38 in her purse and a razor in her garter belt. She's a handful. I never did figure out why Dodie married her."

"He probably knew better than to refuse."

XXXIII

It was almost ten o'clock when Jones parked across the street from the pool room. The lights were still on and the shades were still up. Two guys were shooting at a table at the front, and three were playing a table back in the corner. Bucky was pushing a broom.

Jones pointed through the glass. I know those two: they're Skitch's men, Carlo and Little Tommy. You know those other guys?"

Danny peered through the window. "Jimmy Capuana, Al Briggs, and Eddie Ryan. They're locals."

"Good." He opened the door and went inside.

Bucky looked up from his sweeping. "Hey, Danny. Hey Jones."

"Skitch here, Bucky?" Jones said.

"Yeah. He and Dodie are upstairs. Got a big card game going."

"We need to talk to Skitch." Then to Danny, "I guess you and I better stick around."

"Wanna shoot some pool while we wait?"

"Why not?"

Jones and Danny took a table in the back row. Three games in, the three shooters left. Jones looked out the window and saw a maroon sedan pass under the street light. He turned to Bucky, who was sitting behind the counter. "Hey, Bucky, pull down the shades."

"Huh?" Bucky blinked. "Why? We ain't closed yet."

"Just do it." Jones set his cue on the table and said to Danny. "That maroon Buick's been by here three times in the last five minutes."

No sooner had he said that than the Sight showed Jones the car coming around the block again, fast this time, with gun barrels poking through the open windows.

"Everybody down!"

Outside, the Buick slid to a halt and a spray of machine gun fire shattered the plate glass windows. Carlo and Tommy fell on the first volley.

Crouched behind the pool table, Jones put his hands against the underside of the rail. "Help me," he shouted to Danny. The pair heaved the pool table onto its side. Bullets bounced off the slate. Jones pulled his automatic and fired at the car as fast as he could pull the trigger.

Danny popped up and emptied his revolver through the front windows.

"We're pinned down here," Jones shouted over the chatter of the machine guns and the whine of ricochets. "We've got to move before they throw a grenade through the window."

A burst of gunfire came from above. Skitch and his men were shooting from the third floor; handguns, shotguns and at least one Tommy gun. The Buick roared away with a screech of tires as bullets whanged off its roof. The street was suddenly quiet again.

Danny leaned against the tilted pool table and let out a long breath. "That was close."

Footsteps. Skitch and a half dozen men ran down the stairs, an assortment of guns in their hands. "Jesus Christ Almighty," Skitch said, looking around the room in disbelief. He crouched over Carlo and Tommy. Carlo was still bleeding, Tommy wasn't. "Sam, Billy, Get the Doc. What happened?"

"The bad boys sent us a message," Danny said. "They threw down the glove."

"This was no message," Skitch said. "They didn't just drive by and shoot out the windows." They heard the sound of sirens in the distance.

"You're right," said Jones. "I'm the one they wanted. Drove by a few times to make a positive I.D., then they let loose."

Skitch swore under his breath and said, "I'll kill every one of the bastards."

"That may take some doing. They seem to have a lot of manpower. And before we can take them out, we have to find them. They've been running a game like the Resistance in France. Hide in the shadows, strike when we least expect it. They're the Liberators, we're the occupying force. But there's a difference."

"What's that?"

"We're the hometown boys, not the invaders."

"How do we find them?"

"I think I know a way, but I'd better not be here when the cops arrive." He pulled out his wallet. Jones switched his driver's license with the dead man's. "Let them think I'm dead for a day or two. It'll give me some room to maneuver."

"The cops'll recognize Tommy," Dodie said.

"You're right." Jones picked up a shotgun where it lay on the pool table. He jacked a shell into the chamber. "Stand back."

"What the hell are you doing?" Skitch asked.

"Making sure." He gestured to the corpse. "You don't think he'll mind, do you?"

"Hey, listen, Jones, you can't do this."

"No option." Jones aimed the gun at Tommy's face and pulled the trigger.

"Jesus Christ." said Skitch.

Jones wiped his prints off the shotgun and laid it back on the pool table. "I'll be in touch."

"You're one cold bastard, Jones," Dodie said, staring at him.

He nodded. "Kept me alive up to now." Jones walked to the front door, glass crunching under his feet. He climbed into the roadster, which somehow had escaped damage from the gun battle, and was gone before the first black and white rolled into the square.

XXXIV

ACCIDENT, MARYLAND

Jones pulled the car into a tourist court of twelve log cabin bungalows. The neon sign buzzed "Carter's Log Cabins" and the word "vacancy." Jones had driven through Uniontown and followed Route 40 over the mountains and across the border into Maryland. It seemed far enough away from Brownsville to keep him out of the reach of Blake's men and the cops.

The cabins were arranged in a sort of street, two parallel rows lighted by one shaded bulb on a pole at the far end. Only two of the small cabins had cars parked beside them. A slightly larger one had a lighted sign over the door that said "office." Jones got out and rang the bell. He could see his breath in the cold mountain air. A light came on inside and in a minute, a woman in a blue chenille bathrobe, her hair in rollers, opened the door. "Yeah?" When she opened her mouth to speak, Jones saw she'd taken out her teeth for the night.

"I want to rent a cabin for a couple of days."

"C'mon in."

Jones stepped inside. The cabin was oppressively hot and oxygen starved from the kerosene heater burning in one corner. The inside walls were the same as the outside walls, logs chinked with concrete, giving the inside space a dark, claustrophobic feel. A calendar with a picture of Washington D.C., cherry blossoms in full bloom, hung behind a counter with a register book and a tarnished brass call bell. The tang of liniment hung in the air.

"Ed," the woman called through a curtained doorway. "Got a guest."

"I'm coming." The voice was phlegmy from interrupted sleep. A short, pudgy man shambled through the curtains, pulling his suspenders over his undershirt. Up close, Jones realized that it was he who used the liniment. Ed stepped behind the counter. Open for business. He eyed Jones up and down, and having made his assessment, said, "Two bucks a day, ten for a week."

"Sounds like a bargain." Jones laid a ten on the counter.

Ed held out a fountain pen. "Myra, go get the sheets." Then to Jones, "Just sign the page."

Jones signed the book "William Gable, Pittsburgh."

"You here on vacation?"

"Yeah," Jones said with a chuckle. "I'm taking a vacation from my wife."

"Gotcha," said Ed with a toss of his head toward the curtains.

Myra came back with a pile of bedclothes, sheets, a pillow case, and a blanket that smelled of mothballs. She threw a washcloth and towel on top of the heap.

Ed reached under the counter and pulled out a key on a ring with the number 8 on its fob. "There you go. Heater's full and the bathhouse is up the end of the row."

Jones took the bedding and the key and pulled his car in front of cabin number eight. Jones unlocked the door and stepped in. He pulled the chain for a bare bulb hanging by its cord from the ceiling. The swinging light threw harsh swaying shadows that made the cabin look even bleaker than it might in the daytime. The inside of the cabin was smaller than the office, all but filled with two single beds, a nightstand between them, two chairs and a scarred table with a small Philco radio.

A spider had woven an elaborate web over the head of one of the beds, so Jones took the other. Squatter's rights, he thought. He switched on the radio and it warmed up to the sound of the Tommy Dorsey Orchestra playing "Angel Eyes." Jones didn't bother lighting the kerosene heater. He didn't bother making the bed. He shut off the light and stretched out still dressed on the blue striped mattress. Jones set his automatic on the nightstand beside him, pulled the blanket to his chin, closed his eyes, and quickly fell asleep.

XXXV

Jones woke in darkness. He held the dial of his wrist watch close enough to read the time by the luminous hands: 5:45. The radio was still playing and a droning voice was reporting the prices of corn, lima beans and hogs with the appropriate enthusiasm. He levered himself off the bed and shivered in the morning cold, wishing he'd lit the kerosene heater before he went to sleep.

Outside, an early frost glazed everything that didn't move. The wash house was one room for both sexes, a shower stall and a sink. The heater was burning in the washroom, making it pleasantly warm. Jones opened the taps and as he expected, the faucets were cold and cold. The shower was quick and brutal, but it shook off the cobwebs in Jones's brain as if they were on the end of a cracking whip.

"Mammalian cold water reflex," one of the instructors at Camp X had told the recruits. "Throwback to primitive man; your body thinks you're drowning and pushes all the oxygen to your brain." Testing the theory was never pleasant, but the results were always satisfactory.

As he was toweling off, Myra walked in with a mop and a bucket. Jones pulled the towel over his torso to hide his tattoos and as Myra eyed him up and down, he realized that the towel didn't reach his privates.

"Sorry, Mister," she said, apparently unfazed. "Didn't expect to find anybody in here this early." She shook her head. "No problem. I had three brothers and raised four boys." She turned and walked out the way she came, leaving Jones wondering if her husband pulled the same trick when women were using the shower.

XXXVI

Jones left the cabins and pointed the roadster back into Pennsylvania. He needed his own car and the weapons stashed in its trunk. Just across the state line near Markleysburg, he pulled into a diner called the Chuck Wagon with a twenty-foot wooden cut out of a cowboy towering over it. A cartoon balloon emanating from the cowboy's mouth said, Hungry Podner?" Based on the number of cars and pickup trucks in the gravel parking lot, it was a popular place.

Inside, the Chuck Wagon was busy, although it wasn't quite six thirty and still dark outside. The booths and stools were full of men dressed like farmers, lumberjacks, or truck drivers along with a handful of women dressed like the men. This was the local gathering place for the morning shift.

Jones sat at the counter between a man in a plaid wool hunting shirt and another in a flannel shirt and overalls. The waitress, a hard-bitten type with the beginnings of wrinkled flesh on her forearms, automatically poured him a cup of coffee. No saucer. The spoon stuck out of the cup like one end of a see saw. He'd have to be careful not to put out his eye. "Whattaya want, Bud?"

"Bacon, eggs over easy, and fried potatoes."

"You got it."

The coffee was better than average, strong but not bitter. Jones guessed the clientele emptied the urn before it had time to boil down and turn harsh. A radio was playing behind the counter, but the breakfast conversation drowned it out.

"Bad business in Brownsville last night," someone said three stools down the counter. "Heard there was a gunfight, bunch of people killed, right in town."

"That's what you get with gangsters running the show," another said.

Jones shook his head. By the time the day was over, the rumor mill would have World War Three going on in Fayette County. From what Jones knew of the burgeoning moonshine trade in the county and its constant turf wars with rivals and battles with Revenuers, the hills were no more peaceful than the cities. Who says the grass is greener, he thought.

The waitress set down his plate and a fork. No napkin, no knife. The food was as good as the coffee. While he ate, Jones thought about his next move. If he could find Blake and take him off the board, like cutting the head off a snake, would the whole business collapse? Maybe that would work with an ordinary crew, but these guys were operating on a military model. There was likely a chain of command and a scheme of replacement.

Again, he thought about the Resistance in France. Small independent cells, unknown to each other. It made perfect sense. If one guy gets caught, Collins as an example, he can't rat out people he doesn't know, and he can't spill plans he hasn't been told about. But to run a team with so many players took money. Then there was the issue of military weapons. That took money and connections. Even if he killed Blake, there was no guarantee that such a well organized machine wouldn't keep running, but at the moment, it was his only option.

Jones left a two dollar bill under his coffee cup and walked to the back of the diner where a phone booth sat in the corner outside the rest room door. He dialed Coakee's number. As it rang, Jones imagined the haystack of a man sliding from beneath a car, hauling himself to his feet and crossing the concrete floor of the barn to the unit hanging over the work bench.

"Yeah?"

"It's Jones. How's the Ford?"

"All done. How's the Mercury? Any bullet holes?"

Jones laughed. "Nope, not so much as a scratch."

"I'll believe that when I see it."

"I'll be there in half an hour or so." He hung up.

Jones had to drive way under the speed limit because of the fog, which was actually a bank of clouds too low to clear the mountains, giving him

"It's Jones. How's the Ford?"

the same feeling of flying through them in an airplane. The main difference was that the sky had no obstacles and far less potential for collision.
At any second, a deer could dart out of the trees alongside the road, or a
careless driver could wander over the center line. It took him every minute
of the half hour to reach Coakee's barn, including two missed turns.

The sun was burning through the fog as Jones pulled into the yard.
Coakee's dogs started their usual din, and in a moment, the big man opened
the door to the barn and whistled. The dogs sat quietly and watched Jones
as he climbed out of the roadster. As he crossed the yard to the open door,
the dogs watched him, hoping he would give them an excuse to pounce.

"Anybody ever run afoul of your dogs?" Jones asked.

Coakee chuckled. "Never more than once." He waved Jones inside, and
said. "There she is, Jones, good as new, maybe a little better."

The Ford gleamed under the harsh overhead lights. The bullet holes
were gone, and the window glass was replaced. Jones saw no trace of the
damage.

"You're a wizard, Coakee."

"My boys do good work." He patted the hood. "While it was out of
service, I did a little something to the engine. A fellow named Marlin
Vandermer over in Gibbon's Glade wanted his car set up for dirt track rac-
ing, had the same V-8 as yours. He had some special parts machined for it,
but his luck went bad. Marlin got cancer, and his wife had to sell it all to
pay his doctor bills.

"Long story short, one of the special parts was a cam shaft with longer lobes. A full race cam gives the maximum intake and exhaust, but it
makes the engine idle rough. The one I put in for you, I ground down to
a three-quarter. It ought to boost your horsepower about four to five percent, but she'll still run smooth enough for everyday driving. Not a big
jump in power, but it'll give you a little extra kick when you need it."

"Sounds good."

"You got pretty much the same engine now as Dodie has in that convertible of his." Coakee chuckled. "He even asked me more than once if his
car would be faster than yours."

"Yeah, Dodie's a competitive sort."Jones peeled two hundreds off his
roll and offered them to Coakee. He took one and left the other. "You sure
that's enough?"

"Hell, yeah. Truth be told, I was happy to see her again." He laid a hand
on the fender. "Like visiting one of my kids." He took his hand away and
pulled a rag from his pocket and wiped the handprint from the gleaming

paint. "Treat her right, Jones."

Back on the road, Jones turned on the radio. Rain was falling hard, and the occasional fork of lightning crackled static on the Ford's radio. Count Basie's "One O'Clock Jump" led into the morning news. After a minute about the ongoing withdrawal of U.S. troops from Korea, newscaster Ed Shaughnessy read a cautious report that local police were investigating a shooting in a Brownsville pool room that left one man dead an one injured. No mention of machine guns. Shaughnessy said that the victim's name was C.O. Jones of Los Angeles, California.

The Brownsville cops were sitting on the real story, probably at Skitch's insistence. So far so good. If Blake and his people believed Jones was dead, they wouldn't be watching for him. The word from New Kensington to Skitch, "clean your house," included keeping the State Police and the Feds out of the mix. Eventually, Skitch would have to settle this head-on, and the best help Jones could be was to tilt the odds his way.

The newscast continued and the station played a recording of an impassioned speech on the floor of the Senate. Jones missed the Senator's name at first in the static, but when he spoke, his pronounced Southern drawl made Jones snap to attention. It was the same Cracker dialect Jones heard from Shorty at the High Point.

"And we must root out Organized Crime everywhere it is found before it rots the very underpinnings of American Society with its Hell broth of gambling, drugs, and prostitution," the Senator railed with the vigor and vitriol of a tent Evangelist. "Marijuana, cocaine, and heroin are poisons to the body, the soul and the mind, and we must stop their spread before they drag our young people into the very pit of depravity!"

Shaughnessy followed the recording with, "And that was Senator Orville Robertson of Arkansas introducing a bill to the Senate to expand the powers of the F.B.I. to pursue organized crime."

The rest of the newscast slipped by Jones as his mind began putting together pieces of the puzzle. What was it Collins told them? Blake saying, "Get Robertson to pull all the strings he has to." Who had more strings to pull than a U.S. Senator? Who had easier access to military records to recruit vets for his private army? And who would suspect a crusader against Organized Crime of building a criminal empire of his own? It was a familiar pattern on a different scale: today Brownsville, tomorrow the country.

Time to stop this once and for all.

Jones drove down the mountain into Uniontown and found a phone booth. He dialed the number for the pay phone on the street outside

Danny's apartment. If Danny didn't answer at eight o'clock, he'd keep trying on the half hour 'til he got through. He didn't want to call the pool room number; odds were good that it was tapped, considering the influence the invaders seemed to have. He wished he had Isaac's ear.

Through the glass he could see everyday people hurrying up the sidewalks and driving through busy traffic heading to their jobs. There were days when Jones envied people their ordinary lives, and then he'd ask himself, what would I be? A shoe salesman? A truck farmer? A bricklayer? And he would realize that there was no other life for him than the one he'd been funneled into from the day he was born.

Danny answered on the fifth ring, wide awake. "Hello?"

"It's Jones. Fill me in."

"You heard the radio this morning?"

"Yeah."

"Officially, you're dead. Cops are cooperating, at least for the moment. They're playing it close. Traficante, the undertaker has the body. The story is that Tommy had a beef with you and came into the pool room with a shotgun. The two of you shot it out. Carlo got hit in the cross fire. Tommy killed you and ran for it. Cops have an all points out for his car, but they'll never find it. It's at the bottom of Cheat Lake outside Morgantown."

"Good work all around."

"But everybody's edgy. Skitch has the Coroner and the D.A. in his pocket, but Marano doesn't know how long he can keep the State Police out of it. There's a jurisdictional pissing contest going on, but Skitch has the Governor's ear, and for the moment, the case is strictly local."

"Tell him to keep the lid on as long as he can. I want the opposition to think I'm out of the picture."

"Gotcha."

"See what you can find about the local Armory and call me back at noon at this number." Jones read the number from the dial. "And Danny..."

"Yeah?"

"Watch your back. Nobody says I was their only target."

"I'm flattered."

XXXVII

Jones waited until the early dark to drive into West Brownsville. He parked the Ford two blocks away from Bronski's Grocery and watched the street for five minutes before he opened the door and stepped inside. Janos stood behind the counter, rigid, a nervous tic at the corner of his mouth. "Maria," he called, and Maria Bronski came from the back of the store.

Jones felt his tattoos warming in her presence. He couldn't put his finger on it, but there was something subtly different about her, something at the corners of her eyes and mouth that changed her look from beautiful to sinister. "Are you ready to find our common enemy, Mister Jones?"

"Yes," Jones nodded his mouth suddenly dry.

"You know," she said, "that things done cannot be undone, and you enter this eyes open and willing."

"Yes," Jones repeated. "I understand."

"Then let us go." She held up the bent Coca-Cola cap and stared at it for a moment. "Where is your automobile?"

In five minutes, Jones, Maria, and Janos were driving over the bridge and up High Street, out of town on Bull Run Road and into the wooded countryside near Merritstown. Maria sat in the front seat beside Jones, and he could see her in the dashboard lights, eyes closed, the bottle cap between her fingers.

"Turn left here," she said without looking. Jones did as he was told and left the pavement to find himself on a rutted road paved with "red dog," shale baked by the burning coal piles common to the mines. The road led into a forest of pine trees and looked as if it had been heavily used at one time by trucks and other heavy vehicles, although grass and weeds now sprung up in patches in the humped center. Jones had followed it for another mile or so when Maria said, "Stop the car."

Jones pulled to the side, almost going into a weed-choked ditch.

"The enemy is close. From here, we go on foot."

The three climbed out of the Ford and started walking down the rutted track. In a few moments, Maria stopped and held up her hand. "Here, to the right." There was little moonlight from the clouded sky, but it was enough for Jones to see the outline of a large sign by the side of the road. He switched on his pocket torch and shielded it with his hand as he read, "Columbia Coal, Shaft No. 3" and painted over it with a careless brush the words "No Trespassing."

"He is close," Maria said, "and he is not alone." She led the way through the darkness as if it were as bright as day, but it didn't matter, because her eyes were still closed. The clouds lightened and Jones could make out the hulk of a warehouse-sized building, a machine house for the defunct coal mine. Bricks had been removed from two-thirds of one exterior wall in a pyramid shape to allow the removal of some huge piece of machinery, a generator, Jones guessed.

A sedan was parked near a side entrance to the building. The door stood open, and in the light it threw, Jones could see the silhouettes of two men slouching against the sedan. Neither spoke. The only sound was the low rush of the wind through the tawny weeds.

"You take the one on the left. I'll take the one on the right," Jones whispered. Janos nodded, pulled a knife from his boot, and slipped silently into the darkness. Jones hoped that Maria did not exaggerate her husband's ability.

Jones crept through weeds and cast off hunks of machinery to the corner of the car. Both men were smoking. The one closer to Jones held a rifle by its barrel, the butt on the ground. Suddenly, a voice in his head said, "Now!" He recognized it as Maria's and understood that Janos heard the same command. Both sprang from the darkness at the same instant. Jones caught his target by the head and pulled it back, exposing his neck. A quick slash, and his man was down, blood gurgling from his throat.

Janos stood over his victim, the hilt of his knife sticking out of the man's chest. Jones signaled him to stay, and as he moved toward the doorway, the light inside went out. Jones cautiously stepped into the building. The inside was pitch dark. The floor was concrete and littered with rubble, so he had to feel his way slowly. His fingertips found a wall, which he followed to an open doorway into another room. He counted to ten and eased his way through the opening.

The sight tingled at the base of Jones's skull, but the darkness of the warehouse revealed nothing. He dropped to a crouch, and in a second he heard the "phut" of a silenced pistol and felt the wasp sting of a bullet grazing his ear. He rolled to the side, feeling for cover.

"I see you, Jones." The voice belonged to Blake. "Somehow, I knew you couldn't have died so easily." Jones fired four shots in a fan, aiming toward the place where the voice came from. Slugs ricocheted off the concrete walls.

"Missed," the voice taunted. A second shot grazed the knuckles of

Jones's gun hand. The automatic clattered to the floor. He reached for it, but a third shot hit the pistol and spun it away on the concrete.

"Don't try it. Stand slowly." Jones hesitated. "Oh, come on, Jones. Be sensible. If I wanted to kill you, you'd be dead already."

Jones rose slowly.

"Hands away from your sides."

A match, then the yellow flame of a kerosene lamp. Blake stood across the room, one hand on the lamp and the other holding a Colt revolver, its long barrel extended by a suppressor. Night vision goggles dangled around Blake's neck. He was wearing the same tan suit he wore when he confronted Jones in the diner.

"Step out into the center of the room." Blake's smile was rigid, as if it were carved in oak. "You have a second pistol inside your jacket. Take it out by the handle, thumb and forefinger, and set it on the floor. No tricks. My pistol is aimed a dollar bill south of your navel."

Jones set the .38 on the floor and Blake said, "Now kick it to me." The revolver skittered across the rough concrete.

"You have been something of a mystery to me, Jones, or Lattimer, or whatever your real name might be. My sources searched the OSS records and couldn't find you. Then the light came on. You were one of Hennessey's boys, right? Part of his personal freak show. What was your magical talent?" Blake sneered. "I know it's not seeing in the dark or reading minds. Walking through walls? Talking to the dead?"

Jones gave no answer.

"No boasting? It doesn't matter anyway."

"So what now, Blake? You're going to convert me at the point of a sword?"

"Wishful thinking on your part." He chuckled. "Oh, no, Jones, it's far too late for that." He spun the revolver around his index finger by the trigger guard like a movie cowboy. "You've caused me some delays and some costly problems. You've even managed to track me here. I want the satisfaction of disposing of you myself."

Blake set his pistol on a crate beside him. "I don't want to shoot you, Jones. I want to enjoy this." Blake dropped his left hand, and a dagger with a six-inch blade slid into his palm. "By the way, it was the left hand, Jones."

"What?" Jones felt the blood drip from his ear into his shirt collar.

"The knife was in my left hand in the booth at the diner. And you were right; I had no order to kill you that day, but I do now. I want to do this with knives, so pull out your Ka-Bar and let's get this fight started."

"It's your call, Blake." As Jones reached for the knife in his boot, Blake flicked his wrist. The dagger flew across the room and sunk into Jones's thigh. He gasped in pain.

Blake shrugged, palms up, almost in apology. "I didn't say a fair fight, Jones." He snapped his right arm out, and another dagger shot into his hand. He scraped the edge of the blade across his tongue then held it in his right hand, thumb on the pommel.

Jones pulled the dagger from his thigh and drew his Ka-Bar from its sheath. He held the dagger in his right hand in the same downward slash-and-stab grip as Blake, and the Ka-Bar in his left in a blade-forward thrusting grip. He crouched as Blake sinuously circled him, a balletic fusion of grace and menace casting stark shadows from the lamp onto the brick walls.

In a crouch, Jones turned to follow Blake's narrowing spiral, his injured thigh throbbing and his trouser leg soaking with blood. He was lucky Blake didn't hit his artery, but the leg was weakening fast, and he didn't know how long it would take his weight.

Blake darted in and with a sweeping slash grazed Jones's forehead and danced away, just an inch out of Jones's reach. The cut was calculated, intended to drip blood into Jones's eyes and hamper his vision.

Jones lunged at Blake with a thrust from the Ka-Bar. Blake threw both forearms up, deflecting the thrust with his right forearm, and blocking a slash with his left. He spun and drove his heel into the stab wound in Jones's thigh. Jones grunted in pain.

"Not bad, Jones, but not good enough, either." Blake circled Jones clockwise, knife hand to the inside. He strutted like a toreador, keeping his body edgewise to his opponent, minimizing exposure.

"Who trained you, Jones? Was it Blythe at Camp X? Or was it Donovan? You know," he said, circling, "Donovan trained Blythe. He taught Blythe everything he knows about cold steel combat. Donovan didn't teach Blythe everything he, Donovan knows, but Donovan taught it all to me."

Blake swooped in at Jones, and as Jones raised an arm to block him, Blake flipped his dagger from one hand to the other, and slashed Jones across the back of his neck. "Too slow, Jones," Blake said. "But I expect you"ll get even slower as the fight wears on."

The sight tingled in Jones's head. He saw Blake spin counter clockwise and slash backhand at his throat. Jones threw up a defensive left arm, and at the same time brought the dagger in his right hand across Blake's face, in a scything motion, slashing his cheek, and on the return arc, brought the blade in to stab at his shoulder. The point glanced off Blake's collarbone and he stepped back, startled.

He recovered his composure quickly. He smiled. "Good move, Jones. This is more of a challenge than I expected." He looked down at the drops of blood on his lapel. "Shame about the suit." Blake sprung, and as he shot by Jones, he brought the edge of his dagger across the back of Jones's hand. Jones felt tendons let go, and the Ka-Bar fell to the floor.

It was becoming more difficult for Jones to move. His boot was filling with blood, and his leg was beginning to numb. Blake switched his grip, flipping the knife blade up and began darting in and out at Jones, parrying and thrusting, wounding Jones two tries out of three. Jones felt a wave of vertigo, then his leg collapsed under him and he fell to the floor. Snarling, he raised himself onto one elbow, twisting his torso so that his knife hand was free. Blake stood just out of reach and kicked the dagger from Jones's hand. The knife went spinning into the air to clatter on the concrete.

Jones's eyes swept the room. If only he could reach one of the pistols.

"Oh, Jones, what a waste. You should have joined us when you had the chance."

"You think you're going to topple the Mafia by taking one small town?"

"Brownsville is only the first. The death of a thousand slices, Jones."

"But it really isn't about stopping crime, is it?"

Blake laughed. "That's what the troops think. They believe that they're doing it all for God and Country. At least they did when they joined up. Some of them have figured it out, but they don't give a damn."

"It's really all for Robertson, isn't it? He wants it all."

Blake's eyes widened. "You're sharper than I thought, Jones. I can tell you, since it'll never leave this room. Yeah, Robertson sees the money in the rackets, and the power."

"So he hoodwinks a bunch of vets with a phony crusade to do his dirty work."

"And he greases the wheels behind the scenes." Blake fingered the goggles. "We get the best equipment, and all the money we need from some government slush fund. But enough of that." Blake held the dagger by its tip and pommel between his thumbs and forefingers.

"The question now, Jones, is where will I cut you next?" Blake's smile broadened. "I feel like a god. How you die is all up to me. Do I kill you quickly, or do I kill you slowly and painfully, or do I just open an artery and watch your life pour out? Maybe I'll flip a coin. No magic can help you now."

"There you are wrong."

Blake's head swiveled to see Maria standing in the doorway.

"You. What are you doing here?"

"Bringing justice." She held out her hand and Blake saw the bent bottle cap in her open hand. "Remember?" She said. "Twenty-two ridges. Details are important."

Maria mouthed words Jones couldn't hear, and the bottle cap snapped straight, popping into the air and landing in her palm. Maria spoke again, and the cap began to spin around its axis, ridges gleaming in the harsh light. The spinning cap picked up speed until it made a whistling hum.

Blake stared at the spinning cap, transfixed by the sight. Maria held the heel of her hand to her face, puckered her lips and blew a breath. The spinning cap sailed across the room, and before Blake could shield his face with his hands, it burrowed into his left nostril.

The spinning cap chattered like a dentist's drill in a stubborn tooth, and Blake clawed at his face while chips of bone and gobbets of bloody flesh sprayed from his nose. He screamed in pain and terror and began sawing at his nose with the dagger to dig the deadly cap out of his face. The chatter ceased as the ridges of the cap broke through his skull and entered the soft tissue inside it.

Blake's bulging eyeballs filled with blood. He dropped his knife and stopped clawing at his face as he lost control of his limbs. Pink froth bubbled from his nose and mouth. He flopped on his back, arms and legs thrashing. Finally, he stopped flailing, as one by one, the bubbles burst.

"Janos!" Maria shouted, her voice echoing through the building. She knelt beside Jones and tore a strip of cloth from her skirt. Jones still clutched the dagger in his hand. Maria took it from him and cut away his trouser leg. The blood was flowing steadily, but not spurting. The knife had missed the artery by a scant inch.

Maria made a pad of Jones's trouser leg and pressed it against his thigh. "Hold this." She wrapped the strip from her skirt around the leg and pulled it tight. Janos came in, holding his rifle at the ready. "Help me," she said, and she and her husband pulled Jones to his feet by his armpits. Jones sagged between them, and Janos threw him over his shoulder. The last thing Jones remembered was being heaved into the front seat of the Ford and thinking, I hope I don't bleed much on the upholstery.

XXVIII

Jones woke on a table in the kitchen of the Country Club hideout. Danny was slumped against the sink smoking a cigarette. "His eyes are open."

"Good." Jones turned his head and saw a short man with a fringe of grey hair over his ears and thick glasses preparing a hypodermic needle. He thumbed the plunger and a spurt of fluid shot from the end. The doctor leaned over, putting his face in front of Jones's. "I'm giving you a shot to keep your leg from getting infected."

Jones felt a sharp jab in his thigh. "You were lucky, pal. Another inch and it would have hit your femoral artery, and we wouldn't be having this conversation." Jones heard the rattle of pills in a bottle. "See that he takes one of these every four hours."

"Will do, Doc." Danny said.

The doctor left the room, and Danny told Jones, "Your friends parked your car outside the pool room and honked the horn. By the time a couple of the boys came out, they were down the block and heading around the corner. So, you're still alive. Did the other guy get the worst of it?"

"Blake's dead." Jones shuddered at the memory.

Danny nodded. "And that's how you got this?" Danny held up a bulky olive drab walkie-talkie.

"Janos and Maria must have found it in Blake's car."

"Your friends are a pretty savvy pair."

"They survived the invasion of Poland."

"Good thing you had them along with you."

"Without them, I'd be dead."

Danny turned a dial on the radio, and the volume rose with a crackle of static. "Can't really get much reception down here, but up top I've been listening in. The other team's in a panic looking for Blake. Want to say a few words?"

"No, let them stew a while. Listen and learn. When the time's right, we'll give them a call. I have to talk to Skitch first."

"Yeah, that's a good idea. He's loading the guns for a showdown."

"Can we get him on the phone?"

"No need. He's on his way out here."

"Is that a good idea? Blake had good intel. What if they know about this place? He could be walking into a trap."

"That's possible, but he and Dodie didn't want the town shot up. They figure this place is as good as any for a standoff."

"But we don't know how many men they have, or what kinds of weapons."

"They've thought about that, but they've got a plan."

Jones slipped in and out of consciousness as Danny laid out the details. What he heard sounded risky, but it was as good a plan as any.

"Danny," Jones said. "Don't let me sleep through the fireworks."

"Not a chance. I have a feeling we're gonna need all the guns we can get."

XXXIX

Jones had no sense of night or day in the underground hideout, and his watch lay on a table across the bedroom where Danny and Sal carried him after the doctor finished sewing him shut. Danny left after they put Jones in the bedroom, so he had no one to ask about the time. He tried to turn his head to look for a clock and felt the itching burn of the stitches across the back of his neck.

He felt as if he'd lain there for hours, but the shot of morphine the doctor gave him kept him slipping in and out of consciousness. Jones protested, but the doctor told him, "What I have to do is going to hurt like hell, and I don't want you jerking around and making it more difficult while I do it."

Jones took inventory. When he moved his leg, he felt a deep tissue pain, blunted by the morphine. He ran his fingers over the stitches, counting them;:five on the outside, but with a deep wound like his, there were likely as many inside as well. He held his hand in front of his face. The doctor said he'd need surgery to repair his left hand. He tried to close it into a fist, but only his index and middle fingers would close. That's okay, he thought. I can still pull a trigger.

Twelve stitches closed the slash across his forehead; another scar on his face. Every stroke that Blake delivered was calculated and precise. Jones had to admit, Blake was as good with a knife as anyone he'd ever fought and probably would have killed him if Maria had not stepped in.

Jones tried to sit up, but the morphine got the best of him. He sank back onto the bed. Just have to ride this one out, he thought. Just ride it out.

When he woke the next time, Danny was sitting beside the bed reading a copy of the *Police Gazette*. "I won't bother asking how you feel, Jonesey. I can guess the answer."

"What time is it?"

"Two-thirty." He added, "a.m." He rose from his chair and walked to the doorway. "Hey, Skitch; he's awake."

Skitch came in with Dodie right behind him. "I gotta say, Jones, when I saw you lying there, I was afraid you'd never wake up."

"Live to fight another day," Jones mumbled.

"Huh?"

"My old unit's motto: Live to fight another day. Bottom line, that's all that matters."

"You don't look like you'll be fighting anybody today," Dodie said.

"The hell I'm not. When it's time, I'll be on my feet if you have to prop me with a two-by-four. This isn't the Alamo, and I'm not Jim Bowie."

"Danny showed me the radio," Skitch said. He says we can reach the other side with it."

Jones turned his head toward Danny and winced at the pain. "Did you figure out what frequency they're using?"

Danny nodded. "Two of them. We should be able to connect with them on one or the other."

"What have you heard?"

"They called for somebody named Scorpion—I figure that was Blake— off and on for a couple of hours, then they stopped calling for him, and somebody called Spider started giving orders."

"So they have a chain of command and succession," Jones said. "But it must've rattled them to lose Blake."

"Not as much as losing their cache of ordnance," Danny said. "We went to the warehouse and found two cases of guns and ammo in the trunk of their car. It looks like the Hunt Armory had a clearance sale."

"As well as they seem to have this laid out, I'm betting that's *a* cache, not *the* cache." Jones said.

"Still," Skitch said, "it ought to even up the odds."

"With this crew, we'll need all the evening we can get. We're dealing with professionals here."

"Yeah?" Dodie said, "Well we're pros too."

Jones let the comment slide, but in his head, he was thinking, Yeah, Dodie, but there are pros and then there are *pros*.

After Dodie and Skitch left, Jones asked Danny to help him up. "Get me on my feet. I don't want to fight this battle from bed. Besides, if anybody's going to call those bastards to the fight, it oughta be me, and the walkie won't work in this bunker."

Danny nodded agreement. "You earned the privilege." He held out his hand and Jones gripped it as tightly as he could while Danny pulled him upright. A wave of nausea washed over Jones, and he thought for a minute he was going to puke.

"You okay?" Danny said.

Jones nodded. "It's the morphine. I wish Doc hadn't given it to me."

"But while he was sewing you up, you'd've wished he had."

Jones sat on the edge of the bed, his feet dangling. His thigh was throbbing, a dull ache that would get worse as the hop wore off. "What kind of firepower do we have in the house?"

"Lots of pistols and shotguns and two Tommy guns that Skitch had on hand. The good stuff was in Blake's trunk; eight M-1s and ammo, a few grenades, a flare pistol, and a Browning 1919 with a full belt. But there's more. We've got an M20 bazooka."

"The Super model; nothing but the best for these boys. Who do we have with experience using one?"

"You and me." Danny chuckled. "It'll come in handy if they bring a tank."

"Don't laugh. They seem to have access to just about anything." Jones shook his head to clear it. "Okay. Stand me up."

Danny helped Jones to his feet. Jones thought long and hard before he took a step. He half expected to pitch on his face, but the leg held. "Find me a pair of pants and a cigarette."

XL

Jones and Danny stood on the rocky knob of a hill a quarter mile above the farm. The cold moonlight painted stark shadows from the outcroppings of limestone that pushed through the grass like the knuckles of a giant fist. The air was sharp, and when Jones let out a breath, it looked as if he blew out a lungful of smoke.

Danny pulled the antenna on the walkie-talkie to its full length and switched on the power. "Ready to go." He handed the unit to Jones. "It's set to one of the channels they use."

"The range can't be very far because of the hills."

"A mile or so, if we're lucky."

"We might have to try another location."

"I heard more than one voice when I listened in, so I figure they have units in different places, or maybe a base radio with stronger reception. One of them is bound to hear our signal. It's funny they were looking for Blake. I wonder why they didn't just go to the warehouse."

"We're back to that need-to-know model. Who knows why Blake was there. It looks as if his people didn't know every place he went or every-thing he was doing. The weapons in the trunk of his car give me the idea that they were planning a big move and maybe they were ready to make it."

Static snapped and popped in Jones's ear. He pushed the call button three times and listened. In seconds, a faint voice crackled through the earpiece. "Read you. Over."

Jones said, "This is Scorpion. Over."

There was silence for a full minute before another voice came through the earpiece. "You're not Scorpion. Who is this?" The accent was pure Arkansas.

"Spider, is that you?" Jones said. "This is C.O. Jones." The silence at the other end of the transmission told Jones he was right. "We've had enough of this pissing around. It's time to put up or shut up. We're waiting for you. You know how to read a map." Jones gave him the coordinates for the farm. "Come and get us, if you have the balls."

The radio put a ragged edge on Spider's laugh. "The Country Club. You don't know what you just started, Jones, but we're gonna end it for you." The radio went silent.

"He sounds pretty confident," Danny said.

"They knew about the hideout already. We'd better get back to the house and make sure we're ready for them. In the meantime, keep an ear on the radio. They know we have one now, and if they're smart, they'll stay off the air, but we might get lucky."

Back at the farmhouse, Skitch's men were busy barricading the doors and boarding over the windows. The likeliest direction of attack was from the front of the house. The tree line was less than a hundred yards away and would provide cover. A creek crossed the ground between the house and the trees, but it was no more than eight feet wide and shallow. The stubbled corn field to the rear of the house offered no cover and was well lit by the moon. Also the house faced east, so if the attackers came at sunup or later, the sun would be at their backs.

At Jones's direction, Skitch's men pulled the cars into a rough crescent around the front of the house. When Dino Valllone balked at putting his Oldsmobile in the line of fire, Skitch told him. "If we live through this, hell, I'll buy you a new Cadillac."

"Come and get us, if you have the balls."

"It bothers me that they knew about this place. That means they already know the terrain, and as organized as they are, they probably already have an attack plan," Jones said, checking the ammo belt on the Browning machine gun. It was set in a gable in the attic to cover the front yard and the field beyond to the trees. "I'm glad this house is brick and not wood."

"Or straw," Danny quipped.

Jones laughed. "We've got a lot more than a big bad wolf to hold off."

"Like I was saying."

Eight of Skitch's men took up positions in and around the barn. The rest, eighteen including Jones and Danny, held the house.

"When's sunup?" Jones asked.

"In about an hour," Dodie said."

"They'll attack at dawn," Jones said, "when the sun's in our eyes."

"How do you know that?" Skitch asked.

"Because that's what I'd do."

"Let them come," said Dodie. "We'll give them a fight."

"You know," Danny said, "It won't be over 'til all of them are dead or all of us."

Dodie shrugged. "Occupational hazard."

XLI

Jones sat in the attic window manning the machine gun. Skitch's men were as ready as they could be. They were tough, many of them had killed before, but few of them had shot people who were shooting back at them. The enemy was trained and experienced at this kind of fight.

Footsteps on the stairs. Skitch picked his way across the open joists of the attic floor carrying one of the M-1 carbines. A .38 hung in a shoulder holster in his armpit. He sat beside Jones and peered out of the high window.

"You think they're coming?"

"I'd be more worried if they weren't," Jones said. "That would mean they'd hit us someplace else when we weren't ready for it."

"Yeah, I guess you're right."

"What really worries me is their M.O. They like to lead with some unexpected stunt, catch us off guard. Up to now, it's been hit-and-run, but this time, it's for all the marbles, and I'm wondering what cards they're going to play."

"We're dug in pretty good here."

Jones nodded. "But Spider called this place the Country Club. They knew about it already, and I wonder how much they know about it."

"Like the escape tunnel? It's barricaded. Nobody'll get in that way."

"But if things go south, you might want it open."

Skitch shook his head. "No. We're all in for this. I wouldn't run out on my people and neither would Dodie or Jack. Nobody leaves here 'til we can all walk out the front door." He held out his hand and Jones shook it. "Give 'em hell, Jones." And he was gone, leaving Jones alone at the window.

In the second floor windows, men with rifles waited and watched. Outside, men crouched behind the cars, eyes aching from the strain of staring into darkness. Jones was glad for the confiscated carbines. Shotguns and pistols would be useless until the attackers got close, and Jones intended to see that most of them didn't.

The first light of dawn showed over the hills, a faint yellow wash that threw the landscape into a harsh chiaroscuro, pale ground and dark shadows. The walkie-talkie crackled.

"Jones." He recognized Spider's drawl. "Kiss your ass goodbye." The radio went silent. He strained his ears. No morning birdsongs. They were out there, and they would attack soon.

The sun rose. Then Jones heard it, a low rumble that grew into a snarl. The airplane crested the hills and swooped out of the sun into the valley like a diving hawk. Head on, it was hard to tell for sure, but it looked like a P-51 Mustang. It flew straight toward the house and its machine guns opened up, strafing the semicircle of cars. Jones heard screaming, and looked down to see two of Skitch's men on the ground.

Jones fired back, but wasn't sure whether he'd hit the plane or not. It banked into a wide turn for another pass. This time, it fired on the house, bullets shattering windows and ricocheting off the bricks. Jones threw himself backward and almost fell between the floor joists as bullets from the airplane blew chunks of wood from the attic window casement.

He pulled himself back to the windowsill and looked to the tree line. He saw the attackers coming. Rows of them in olive drab field gear and helmets. Jones didn't have time to count heads, but his trained eye told him that there were at least twice as many of them as there were defenders, maybe more crossing the open ground toward the creek bed while the plane kept Skitch's men pinned down.

The Mustang circled for another pass, and as it flew head on toward the house, Danny rose behind one of the cars, the bazooka on his shoulder.

Dodie fed the launcher from behind and slapped Danny on the shoulder.

Shots from the trees—snipers. A bullet caught Danny in his hip and twisted him sideways, but he stayed on his feet long enough to fire the bazooka, and the rocket flew into the Mustang, catching it just behind the propeller. The plane exploded in a spectacular ball of orange flame, and everyone ducked as shrapnel spun in every direction. Parts of the plane, a wing, a rudder, a chunk of the fuselage, sailed through the air. The engine crashed through the roof of the house behind Jones and fell through the ceiling into the room below.

On the ground, the invaders were closing on the creek bed where they could fire from the cover of the bank. Once dug in there, they had the advantage of more rifles with greater range and accuracy. Jones swung the Browning toward the upper end of the creek where Skitch's men had hidden a drum of gasoline for the tractor in the weeds.

A burst from the machine gun riddled the drum, and gasoline poured from a dozen holes into the creek. Jones cocked the flare pistol and fired. A ball of blazing phosphorous arced through the air and came down into the creek, igniting the fuel. Yellow flame swept down the creek as the gasoline, floating on top of the water, exploded. Men swarmed over the bank to escape, many of them on fire.

The barn door rolled open, and a big black sedan roared out. It bounced over the rough ground toward the creek, men with Tommy guns firing from the windows and dropping the attackers until one of them threw a grenade through the sedan's window. Skitch's men jumped from the car seconds before the grenade exploded, reducing the sedan to a heap of twisted steel.

Over the gunfire, Jones heard a grating rumble. A half-track burst from the trees, its mounted .50 caliber machine gun spewing fire. Behind it, another thirty men or more followed on foot. In less than a minute, the half-track was across the creek and heading for the car barricade.

Jones fired the Browning at the half-track, but hit only two of the people in it. The driver aimed it between two of the cars and crashed through, pushing one aside and overturning another. The half-track ran up the steps and onto the porch, collapsing the portico, and Jones felt the impact as it slammed against the wall below him, breaking through into the front of the house.

The driver reversed the half-track and rammed the house again, breaking through the front wall, but someone threw a grenade into the tread on the left, leaving it dragging in a slow arc as the driver tried to back out of the hole he'd made.

Jones aimed the Browning into the half-track but held his fire when he saw Dodie vault the side, and empty his pistol into the driver and two others. The machine gun operator had fallen from the half-track when the grenade went off. He was scrambling back into the vehicle when Skitch fired his carbine and he fell to the ground.

Dodie spun the machine gun around and shouted "*Scendere!*" Duck.

Skitch's men knew the word and fell to the ground. Dodie opened fire on the advancing soldiers, who scattered in every direction. He held down the trigger and sprayed a continuous fire as spent shells flew glittering in the rising sun. "Yeah!" he screamed. "Yeah! Eat that you bastards!"

Jones fired the Browning until the belt ran out, and the attackers kept coming. Another wave burst from the trees. They were almost to the creek when they began falling from a deadly crossfire.

Jones saw them then, advancing over the hills, an army of a hundred or more, many of them with one leg, one arm, carrying deer rifles, shotguns, pistols, a rag-tag army wearing bits and pieces of uniforms, a corps of hometown boys.

He grabbed a shotgun and limped across the attic to the stairs. Jones clambered down them to the second floor in time to see three of the invaders coming up the back stairwell from the kitchen. Jones's first shot caught the point man in the chest and sent him backward taking the other two with him. The second man, using the dead one as a shield, fired an automatic at Jones, who barely had time to scramble for cover. The third ducked out of sight, into a doorway below.

He reached the shotgun around the corner and fired down the stairwell, then pulled his pistol with his left hand. Jones rolled across the opening and took his shot as the man behind the corpse angled for one of his own. His aim was good, and he caught Jones in his left shoulder, but Jones's aim was better. His shot went through the gunman's forehead and spattered the wall behind him with blood and brains.

The third man reached around and fired a machine gun up the stairs. Plaster and splinters peppered Jones as he crouched around the corner.

"That shotgun won't help you now, Jones." The voice. It was Spider. Jones could see his shadow as the leader hid behind the wall.

"Guess again." Jones fired the shotgun, and the pumpkin ball shell he'd loaded for a third shot blew through the lath and plaster. The shadow went flat, and Jones heard Spider fall to the floor.

Outside, the gunfire was dying down to random shots, finishing off the last of the invaders. Jones limped down the stairs, automatic at the ready, but when he turned the corner, ready to fire, he saw Spider, the man in the hat from the High point who drove the car through Bronski's grocery store, propped against the wall under one of the tall windows. The front of his jacket was soaked in blood.

"You won, Jones—this time." He coughed and blood dribbled down his chin. "But there will be others after me." He raised his hand as he coughed again, and the Sight showed Jones what he was about to do, but as Jones tried to cross the room to stop Spider, his leg gave out and he tumbled to the floor.

The cyanide worked quickly, and in seconds the leader was dead.

The gunfire stopped. An eerie silence lay over the valley. Jones dragged himself down the stairs and past the wrecked half-track. The farm was a pastoral scene from hell. Smoke drifted across the shallow vale from burning cars and a half dozen grass fires. Bodies were strewn across the field, and wreckage lay everywhere.

Jones picked up a fallen M-1 and used it as a crutch to limp across the yard where Danny lay on a throw rug somebody brought from inside the house. He was holding a blood soaked pad against his hip and smoking a cigarette.

Jones tried to sit and ended up sprawling on the grass beside him. The pair lay on their backs looking up at the sky.

"How bad is it?" Jones asked.

Danny let out a lungful of smoke. "I won't be doing the mambo any time soon. Six inches to the left, and I'd just tell them to shoot me now and get it over with. How about you?"

Jones touched the back of his neck and his hand came away bloody. "I think I pulled out every stitch the doc put in me. That was a hell of a shot you made, taking down the Mustang."

Danny grinned. "It was him or me. I'm glad I hit him before he dropped a bomb on us."

"*Vivez pour combattre un autre jour.*"

"Huh?"

"Live to fight another day."

Danny nodded. "Good advice."

A spatter of gunfire erupted in the woods across the creek then as abruptly as it started, it stopped. "Sounds like the militia's rooting out the last of them," Danny said.

"Skitch took a big chance relying on the hometown boys."

Danny shook his head. "Naah, he knew they'd come through. He's always taken care of his town and his people. They were just returning the favor. Besides, they know what they've got with him, for better or for worse."

Across the yard, Skitch and Dodie were going man to man, seeing who was hurt and how badly, and getting them the attention they needed. A makeshift triage hospital was set up in the barn, and the worst wounded were being carried in for attention.

Skitch came over with four of the townies. "Take Hayes over to the barn." The men each took a corner of the rug and lifted Danny. "Jones, you're bleeding."

He propped himself on his elbows and Skitch pulled him into a sitting position by his shoulders. "Not from anything new." When Skitch turned his head, Jones saw blood oozing in a slow drip from the top of his ear. "Looks like you caught one."

"Just a nick. It'll give me a touch of class, like a dueling scar in the Old Country. It's a story I can tell for the next twenty years."

"How many did we lose?"

"Eight. Jackie's gonna need a new driver. They thought it would be easy, didn't they?"

"Maybe not easy, but they never thought it would be this tough."

Skitch stuck out his hand. "You're a good soldier, Jones. You followed my orders. You gave 'em hell."

More of the hometown crew trooped into the yard. Jones saw Moe in his garrison cap, a double-barreled shotgun over his shoulder, the kid with the missing hand from the grocery store, a five-dollar nickel-plated .38 stuck in his belt, Herman carrying an old breech loader, and Janos Bronski with his rifle. Jones realized at that moment that this is what Hitler would have found if he'd tried to land on the shores of England.

Jones heard the rumble and clatter of the tractor from the barn and saw Edgar back it into the yard to hitch a tow chain to the overturned car and pull it upright. When he dragged it aside, Jones saw his Ford. The tires were flat on the driver's side and there was no glass in any of the windows. He could only imagine the bullet holes, enough to keep Coakee busy for a week.

"Jones."

He turned his head and saw Jenny Matthews standing over him. She was wearing dungarees tucked into lace-up boots, and a tawny canvas hunting jacket. A Mauser rifle with a long scope hung from her shoulder by a webbed sling.

"Pardon me if I don't stand up."

"You look like hell, but still, better than average for a dead man."

"And, given the situation, you look perfect." He looked around. "Where's your brother?"

"Back at the station with the rest of the cops. He wanted to come, but Skitch asked them to sit this one out. What you can't see, you can't say." She lit a cigarette and stuck it in Jones's mouth. "See you around, Jones."

Believe it, he thought, as soon as I can stand up by myself.

Edgar dragged the half-track away from the front of the house, bringing down a shower of bricks and half the second floor. What was left of the roof sagged in the middle and looked as if it would collapse any second.

Someone had brought the chairs and table from the farmhouse kitchen, and Skitch and Dodie sat in the noon sun with Jones and Jack, passing around a bottle of bourbon and a box of crackers from the pantry.

"What'll we do with that thing?" Mozzo said, pointing at the half-track.

"Once the sun's down, we haul it to the old Vesta four mine and sink it in the settlement pond," Dodie replied, "same with the pieces of the airplane."

"I hate to lose the Country Club," Skitch said. "It was useful."

"But it's been compromised," Jones said. "Blake and his men knew about it, so you can figure their boss knows about it too. But it will make a good mausoleum." Over Skitch's shoulder, Jones could see men dragging corpses into the ruined house and down the stairs into the secure hideout.

Dodie picked up the walkie-talkie. "How do you turn this thing on?"

Jones thumbed the power switch. "Push this button to talk."

Dodie put the handset to his ear and pushed the button. "This is Dodie Mottola. Whoever's listening out there, you can kiss my ass."

XLII

A week later, Jones went back to the pool room for the first time since the battle at the farm. The pool room windows were replaced with new glass, and the locals were back to shooting pool as if nothing had ever happened. Jack Mozzo sat in his usual chair, presiding over the action.

Jones's stitches were out, and he was walking with a cane now, instead of crutches, but the stairs to the second floor still gave him trouble.

On the fourth floor, men were scurrying around the tables piled with policy slips. Business as usual. Dodie waved him over to Skitch's office, and they went inside.

"We won, but some of them got away." Skitch opened the bottom drawer of his desk and pulled out a bottle of Seagrams and three glasses. He poured three shots, one for Jones, one for Dodie, and one for himself.

"You never get them all."

"But they won't try that again." Dodie said. He knocked back his shot.

"Not the same way, anyway," Jones said. "They lost a lot of men including the brains of the outfit, and the foot soldiers who really believed they were on a crusade against evil, found out that having right on your side doesn't make you a winner. I imagine the survivors are demoralized."

"I don't think they'll try again, either," Skitch said, "but this makes me sweat." He laid a newspaper on the desk. The headline read: Senator Blasts Organized Crime. The photo showed Senator Orville Robertson pounding a podium, his mouth twisted in a snarl.

"Senator Robertson called organized Crime, 'a cancer that gnaws at the entrails of civilized society, and one that must be excised by the full might of law enforcement,'" the article read.

"People are talking about running this guy for President," Skitch said. "If he can't take over with his private army, he'll try to take us down with the FBI for revenge."

"What does New Kensington have to say about it?" Jones asked. "How far do their arms reach?"

Skitch shook his head. "They have connections in D.C., but they aren't enough to muscle this guy. He's got too much backing, including the papers and the radio. Take him out right now, it'll make him a martyr, and the finger'll point right at the Mob."

"That way he loses, but so do we." Jones said. "We need to stop him without putting a bullet in his head. I think I know a way."

XLIII

The next day, the spring bell rang as Jones stepped through the door of Shrenk's shop. He was at the counter, dismantling the tumbler set from an office safe. The cadaverous man looked up from his work long enough to identify his visitor then went back to picking at the cams and levers of the lock. "Good day, Mister Jones. What may I do for you?"

"A question for you: in which concentration camp did you serve the Third Reich?"

Shrenk continued picking at the innards of the lock. "I don't know what you are talking about, Mister Jones. I was a prisoner at Auschwitz until your American Army liberated us."

He's a cold one, Jones thought. He laid a page torn from an oversized magazine on the counter and turned it so that Shrenk could see it right side up. It showed a group of Nazi officers posing with Hermann Goering. "The third man from the left is Oberst Rudolph Vandeberg, one of Germany's foremost mechanical engineers before the War. You dyed your hair, put on a yarmulke, and counterfeited a concentration camp tattoo."

Jones's hand clamped on Shrenk's wrist, and he pulled up his sleeve. "I've never seen a concentration camp tattoo so meticulously inked. Your ego just wouldn't allow you the sloppy job the camps did on the prisoners; like everything you do, the craftsmanship had to be perfect."

Shrenk slid his free hand to the edge of the counter. "Don't bother." Jones took a small automatic from his pocket, pointed at Shrenk's left eye and thumbed back the hammer. "I was in here last night while you were asleep and found this little toy under the counter."

"So, Mister Jones," Shrenk said coolly, "What are you going to do? Kill me? Turn me over to the authorities?" His eyes were level, and his hands were perfectly steady.

Jones shook his head. "Nothing so easy. It occurred to me that I should take you to the local synagogue and let the congregation mete out justice. I understand that being stoned to death is particularly unpleasant."

"You followed orders, Mister Jones, as did we all."

"The only reason I haven't blown the whistle on you, Vandeberg, is that I think you'll be useful. Do what I tell you, and your secret is safe, and you can walk away from here with your life and whatever you can load in your car. I need you to build something for me."

XLIV

Jones adjusted the bow tie for the third time since he'd taken the waiter's uniform from the man he left unconscious in the alley behind the garbage cans. The short mustard colored jacket over the pleated shirt and cummerbund had room enough to hide a lightweight shoulder rig, but the tie was strangling him.

In the holster, he carried the weapon Shrenk/Vandeberg had made for him, a compact compressed air pistol that fired a brass filament finer than a human hair. Hennessey had shown him one once when he was an OSS trainee.

"It's simple, really," Hennessey explained. "The gun fires these." He opened his palm, and Jones could barely see what looked like tiny fibers. Hennessey offered a magnifying glass, and on closer inspection, Jones saw that they were the color of brass. "They're made of a special alloy."

He handed Jones the pistol. It was palm-sized and looked almost toy-like. The only feature that looked like it belonged to a pistol was the full sized trigger and guard. Otherwise, the structure of the weapon looked like the spear guns Navy frogmen used, a barrel with a pinpoint bore over a cylinder the size of Jones's thumb.

"Compressed air," said Hennessey, tapping the cylinder. "Fire the filament into the right spot in the target's neck, and it enters the venous system. Eventually, it finds its way into the chambers of the heart and does fatal damage. The filament is too small to be easily detected by an autopsy, if at all, and to all appearances, the target has died of a heart attack."

"And the pistol works?" Jones said.

Hennessey replied with no expression, "It has been tested." He added, "Successfully. The key is getting the filament into the exterior jugular vein. The subject feels nothing more than a pinprick, and the filament is so fine that it leaves no discernable wound. Ideally the filament should be introduced into the subclavian vein in the chest, but that's difficult unless you catch the target in the bathtub or at the beach. The jugular is a much easier target. The gun is all but silent. The risk lies in getting close enough for accuracy."

It took Vandeberg only three days to build a similar weapon. Jones got the impression that the locksmith had built one before.

The ballroom of the Ambassador Hotel, one of Washington D.C.'s finest, was filled to capacity with the gowned and tuxedoed Who's Who of D.C. society to honor Senator Orville Robertson of Arkansas for his crusade against Organized Crime.

The fete was sponsored by the Liberty and Justice Foundation, an arm of the Daughters of the American Revolution, organized to promote law enforcement and anti-crime legislation, another major piece of which Senator Robertson was about to introduce at the start of the Senate's next session.

Jones stepped behind the head table of dignitaries carrying a pitcher of ice water in his left hand and a hand towel in his right. Dinner was finished, and as the guests dug into their pecan pie, Jones moved down the table refilling the glasses of Congressmen, Cabinet members, and their wives.

As he poured water into the glass of Robertson's wife Barbara, a dowdy, white-haired maven, his hand slipped under his jacket and came out with the air-gun hidden under the towel. As he stepped behind the Senator, Jones's index finger curled around the trigger.

Jones stepped behind the seat of honor and fired the weapon. The click of the mechanism and the faint hiss of compressed air were swallowed by the chatter of the crowd and the clink of glasses and silverware. When Robertson's hand rose to touch his neck, Jones knew he had hit his mark. Robertson drew his hand away, looked at his fingertips, and turned back to his dessert.

"More water, sir?" Jones said.

"Uh, no," Robertson replied with a shake of his head. "Thank you, son." The Senator leafed through the notes of the hell-fire speech he was about to deliver. Jones moved on to the end of the head table then slipped through the curtains behind the dais. He set the pitcher on a serving cart and picked up a garbage can full of table scraps. No one paid attention as he carried the heavy can into the alley and ducked into a dark doorway to trade the waiter's uniform for his street clothes.

From the open door, Jones heard boisterous applause from the dining room. Senator Orville Robertson would be stepping up to the podium to deliver what would be his most memorable speech to the assembled dignitaries and to the broadcast microphone that would garner nationwide support for his phony crusade.

Around the block, a burgundy Packard sedan waited at the curb. Jones opened the passenger door and slid onto the front seat.

"How'd it go?" Danny said.

"We'll know soon." Jones turned on the radio, and as they rolled away from the curb into the D.C. traffic, he turned the dial until he heard, instead of music, the stentorian voice of the Senator.

"And I say again," he boomed, "that the mobster is a greater threat to America than any Communist. At least the Communist is motivated by an ideal, an ideology. The mobster is motivated by nothing more than raw greed. He... He..." Robertson's voice trailed off. "My heavens," he gasped into the microphone. "Help me. Help me."

Jones heard startled voices in the background. "Senator, are you all right?" "What's happening?" and Barbara Robertson's frightened, "Orville, what's wrong?"

There was a crash as Robertson pulled the podium over with him and the microphone fell to the floor. A murmur of voices rose to a sea of panic.

"Doctor! We need a doctor here!" someone shouted. "Shut off that microphone." The silence as the air went dead was abrupt, followed after a few seconds by the voice of a studio announcer. "Ladies and gentlemen," he said, "we are experiencing a problem with our broadcast. Please stand by."

A pianist in the network studio struck up a piece that Jones recognized as Brahms then followed with one by Mozart. Then the announcer came on again. "Ladies and gentlemen, we have just received word that Arkansas Senator Orville Robertson has taken ill at the Washington D.C. Liberty and Justice Foundation dinner being held in his honor. Please stay tuned for further details."

Jones switched off the radio. "I guess it went okay."

Danny nodded and aimed the Packard for Pennsylvania.

XLV

Fiddle's was full the next morning when Jones went in for breakfast. He'd passed Shrenk's shop on his way and found the place empty. When he looked in the front window, he saw that all the shelves were bare. He imagined the fugitive Nazi cramming everything he could carry into his Chevy in the dead of night and running for his life. Jones took a seat in a booth as two workmen rose to leave. Mabel came with coffee as he unfolded his newspaper.

"That's something about that Senator, huh? Died on the radio." She pointed to the headline on the front page of Jones's newspaper: Nation Mourns Fallen Senator. The press photographer who got the shot of Robertson falling sideways and dragging the podium with him would probably win a Pulitzer for the picture. It captured the startled eyes and the pained rictus of the man who would be king turned into Humpty Dumpty in a heartbeat, literally and figuratively.

Jones shrugged. "'Time and chance happeneth to them all.'"

Mabel frowned. "You sound like my minister, like we're all doomed or something." She moved on with the coffeepot, and Jones skimmed through the article. It reported that "Senator Orville Robertson had succumbed to a heart attack while delivering a speech in the Nation's Capital." The piece was filled with praise from colleagues and officials including a statement from FBI Director J. Edgar Hoover, probably written by a staff member, who stated that Robertson's "unwavering support for law enforcement would be greatly missed." Hoover, who publicly denied that the Mafia even existed, was probably breathing a sigh of relief along with every mob boss from Jersey to Vegas. The paper printed the full text of Robertson's speech on an inside page, but Jones didn't bother reading it; he'd heard enough of it the night before.

"Hey, Jones."

He looked up from the newspaper and saw Jenny Matthews standing beside the booth. Today, she was wearing dark slacks and a grey pullover sweater. Her honey blond hair cascaded over her shoulders and framed a face accented by subtle touches of lipstick and eye shadow. She looked around. "Place is full; nowhere to sit."

Jones didn't answer.

"For Chrissakes, Jones, are you going to invite me to join you, or do I have to eat my breakfast standing up?"

Jones laughed and waved to the empty side of the booth. "Be my guest." She sat, and Mabel hurried over with coffee. Her eyes betrayed amusement as she said, "One check?"

"Yeah," Jenny said before Jones could open his mouth. "My turn, Jones. I owe you a breakfast." Mabel took their orders and scurried to the kitchen.

"I feel like I've been set up."

"Good instincts," Jenny replied.

"What about your brother?"

Jenny stirred her coffee. "When word came that Roger wasn't coming home, Rudy told me he'd be my guardian angel until I found someone to watch out for me. Want the job?"

"I don't come cheap. Besides, I already have a job working for Skitch."

"You'd only have to work nights for me." She smiled, and for the first time, Jones saw all the perfect teeth that lay behind those lips.

"Deal."

THE END

ABOUT OUR CREATORS

AUTHOR –

FRED ADAMS JR. is a retired Penn State University English Professor who spends his days writing pulp fiction and his nights working as a singer-songwriter. His novel *Dead Man's Melody* was nominated as Pulp Novel of the Year in this year's Pulp Factory Awards. Airship 27 Productions has published a number of his novels since 2014 and has more waiting in the wings. His titles include: *Hitwolf* 1 and 2, *Six Gun Terrors* vol. 1 and vol. 2, C.O. Jones series *Mobsters and Monsters; Skinner; The Damned and the Doomed;* and *Hometown—U.S.A,* as well as the horror pirate tale *Fangs of the Sea*. He also contributes to Airship 27's anthologies. His original Sherlock Holmes anthology *The Affair of the Chronic Argonaut* was recently published by Pro Se Press. He lives in Mount Pleasant, Pennsylvania and describes himself as living "in perpetual terror of boredom."

ARTIST –

ROB DAVIS began his professional art career doing illustrations for role-playing games in the late 1980's. Not long after he began lettering and inking, then penciling comics for a number of small black and white comics publishers- most notably for Eternity Comics, which eventually became Malibu Comics in the 1990's, on their book SCIMIDAR with writer R.A. Jones. Branching out to other black and white publishers and eventually working at both DC and Marvel Rob worked on likeness intensive comics like TV adaptations of QUANTUM LEAP and STAR TREK's many incarnations mostly on the DEEP SPACE NINE comics for Malibu. At Marvel he worked on the Saturday morning cartoon adaptation PIRATES OF DARK WATER. After the comics industry implosion in the late 1990's Rob picked up work on video games, advertising illustration and T-shirt design as well as some small press comics like ROBYN OF SHERWOOD for Caliber. Rob continues to do the odd self-published comic book as well as publisher and designer for his small-press production REDBUD STUDIO COMICS. Rob is Art Director, Designer and Illustrator for the New Pulp production outfit AIRSHIP 27 partnered with writer/editor Ron Fortier. Rob is the recipient of the PULP FACTORY AWARD for

"Best Interior Illustrations" in 2010 and 2015 for his work on SHERLOCK HOLMES: CONSULTING DETECTIVE and has been nominated for the same award nearly every year. He works and lives in central Missouri with his wife and two children.

— — —

BOOKS BY FRED ADAMS JR.

FRED ADAMS JR. PULP WRITER

SIX-GUN TERRORS Volume One
SIX-GUN TERRORS   Volume Two
SIX-GUN TERRORS Volume Three – The Slithering Terror

HITWOLF
HITWOLF 2 – The Pack

C.O. JONES—Mobsters and Monsters
C.O. JONES—Skinners
C.O. JONES – The Damned and the Doomed
C.O. JONES—Hometown—U.S.A.

(SAM DUNNE MYSTERIES)
Dead Man's Melody
Blood is the New Black

(THE SMITH BROTHERS SERIES)
The Eye of Quang Chi

(IKE MARS MYSTERIES)
The Bloody Key
Wired

FANGS OF THE SEA

SEAS of HELL

At the height of the Spanish Inquisition, a large number of the faithful fled Spain and the corrupted church to find haven and new lives on a chain of small islands south of Cuba. There, under the guidance of their priest, Father Beppo, they established peaceful fishing villages that would sustain them in both body and soul. It was their small piece of an earthly heaven.

Then black sails appeared on the horizon, furled from the masts of an unholy ship called Votrelec and captained by Varleck, a vampire pirate. Ever on the hunt for fresh bodies to man his crew of the undead, the blood hungry monster is delighted when discovering the unprotected islands. He is overconfident in his dark powers. Soon he realizes the villagers, under the guidance of the old cleric, have no intention of succumbing to his monstrous will. And so the endless battle of good versus evil is joined. But who will emerge victorious and who will fall when the seas run red with blood?

FANGS of the SEA

Fred Adams Jr.

AN AIRSHIP 27 PRODUCTION

PULP FICTION FOR A NEW GENERATION!

AIRSHIP27HANGAR.COM

NEW PULP

www.ingramcontent.com/pod-product-compliance
Lightning Source LLC
Chambersburg PA
CBHW051150260626

47170CB00005B/2042